BROWNING SAHIB

BROWNING SAHIB

A Browning adventure in old Ceylon

Peter Corris

For
Geoff and Nancy Sawer

David Stratton, film historian and critic, helped greatly with the research for this book. As always, Jean Bedford has encouraged me, provided ideas and civilised the manuscript.

P.C.

CHAPTER ONE

I think it was Gary Cooper who said something like, 'In twenty years as a movie actor, I spent one year acting and nineteen waiting to act.' In the years after the Second World War I seemed to spend more time in travelling to get somewhere to act than at acting. It wasn't just a matter of being on location, although I had my share of that—I was in Kenya with Stewart Granger and Deborah Kerr to do a few scenes in *King Solomon's Mines*, for example—but because I was criss-crossing the Atlantic to work in British and American pictures. I had smallish character parts in things like *Crossfire* and *Quo Vadis* (who didn't?) and *Viva Zapata!* in the States, and in *The Winslow Boy* and *The Wooden Horse* and *The Lavender Hill Mob* in Britain.[1] There were others, where I hardly spoke at all, that I've forgotten. More often than not I was in uniform. You see, I could play an American, a Britisher or an Australian (as I did in *The Wooden Horse*), and I'd kept my hair and more or less kept my figure, so that I didn't look my age.

Mind you, I was no Peter Pan. I looked as if I'd been around a bit, survived a war and a few battles with blondes and bottles. All this was true. But in fact I'd survived *two* wars, which was something I kept very dark. It's a matter of luck. I'd eaten and drunk my fill and smoked and bed-hopped for longer than I would've admitted to anybody, but I was holding together. Activity has a good deal to do with it. I've always been keen on certain sports—tennis and horse-riding in particular—and they help you keep the flab at bay.

Anxiety plays a part, too. For some reason, I've never managed to achieve financial security and there's nothing like money worries to trim you down. To tell the truth, money had something to do with my many Atlantic crossings. In those days, before computers and faxes and all that nonsense, if you ran up a debt in a Soho gambling club or got into trouble with your Bel Air rent, a quick hop across the briny could be a big help.

As I say, I had the looks for the work. I'm a big chap, but not so big as to dwarf any reasonable-sized leading man (nothing you could do about Ladd, Bogart, Cagney and company, of course, except bend your knees and stay in medium or long shot). In tweeds I was an Englishman, in seersucker a Yank and I could be any kind of colonial they wanted. Also in my favour was the fact that the movies were a little short on presentable masculine actors at that time. The brooding boys like Brando and Dean were just coming in and some of the old hands were getting a bit long in the tooth. If you wanted a well set up fellow on a horse or leading a safari or hanging onto the wheel of a ship in a gale, I could be your man. For one thing, my hair wouldn't fall off.

I could be had cheap, too—we all could, apart from the top-liners. After 1950, when some anti-trust law stopped the studios actually owning the theatres, movie production in America was cut back. Television was starting to threaten the box office takings and the unions that had grown stronger during the war were flexing their muscles. They wanted better rates and conditions for caterers, animal-handlers, set-builders and drivers—all people the studios had treated like dirt in days gone by. Studio contracts for character actors were becoming a thing of the past, and even the stars were loaned out and traded like baseball players. My agent, N. Robert Silkstein, kept me in work by applying some of the simple philosophy he had learned in twenty years of rooting around in the Hollywood garbage pile.

'Dick,' he said, 'if you're gonna have to see someone again, be nice. If you ain't, screw 'em.'

Bobby Silk was nice to Selznick (which I found it impossible to be) and Hitchcock and Korda (the English were still riding a post-war wave) and their casting directors, and I made commissions for him and a living for myself. It wasn't such a bad life. By playing cards on the boat there was always the chance of picking up a few extra pounds on the way over, and dollars on the way back. American cigarettes fetched great prices in London and English socks sold for three times the price in LA. Nor was it all just buck-turning: if you've ever travelled as a single man on a comfortable passenger ship (provided you're interested in such things) you'll know that there are many romantic opportunities with bored wives, new widows, adventure-seeking secretaries and the like. There's a saying in the movie business that 'it isn't adultery if it's on location'. In my experience, much the same goes for if it's on board ship.

So when I arrived in London in the autumn of 1952 to do some work on *The Cruel Sea* (more double-breasted uniformed stuff), I was in reasonable spirits after winning a few hands of poker and having a good romp with the Honourable Pamela Price-Austin, who was returning home to marry Sir Stanley Someone-or-other after touring the USA with her American-born mother. Sexually, stay-at-homes are a write-off. Shake a woman loose from her moorings, I always say, and you'll get a true idea of her character. The only problem for me on the voyage had been choosing between the mother and the daughter, and fending off the one after I'd settled on the other.

I said my goodbyes to the Hon. Pam at Tilbury, where she and Lady Donna Price-Austin had a Rolls waiting, and hopped on a bus for Piccadilly.

It never took me long to settle back into London life. After all, I'd been visiting the place since my undistinguished career in the First AIF,[2] and, apart from being terribly belted around in the Second World War, the old place doesn't change much. There was still a lot of that damage in evidence in 1952 but the bargains in real estate, which had made some quick-off-the-mark types very rich, had all gone, worse luck. Not that I'd ever had the capital to get in on that game. Money, in fact, was in somewhat short supply for the moment despite my boat winnings. I had ten cartons of Lucky Strikes in my suitcase. Smuggled in, of course, and not the faintest whiff of a problem because I'd stuck very close to the Hon. Pam and her Ladyship as we went through customs and they just chalked my bag and waved me on. But until I'd translated them into cash and got on the payroll I'd have to watch the pennies.

Most of my scenes were being shot on a boat in Portsmouth Harbour. Portsmouth's a jolly enough place at that time of the year—good pubs, some decent parties and dinner dances, a bit of tennis and golf—but I wasn't due there for a few days and planned to kick up my heels in London. You could have fun without a lot of money if you knew the right people, and I did. I installed myself in the Regent and had a word to Simon Bentley, an assistant manager, who got a kick and a quid out of disposing of my contraband. I unpacked, had a long bath and a stiff scotch, and got on the telephone.

'Rex, it's Dick Browning.'

'I'm sorry, Mr Browning. Mr Harrison is presently in the United States.'

'This is Richard Browning. Could I please speak to Michael Wilding.'

'Mr Wilding and Miss Taylor are in Scotland, Mr Browning. They are not expected back until the end of June.'

It was the first I'd heard of it. Mike, hitched up to the luscious Liz? He must have been twenty years older than her. Well, good luck to him.

I knew Judy Garland was in town and I knew she'd be staying at the Savoy. I rang and was put through to her husband and manager, Sid Luft. 'Sid? Dick Browning. Yeah, I just hit town and I figured you'd know where the action is tonight.'

'Not tonight, Dick. She's down.'

'Take her out. Liven her up.'

'Not tonight. I've got to get her fit to sing in three days. It's gonna be a full-time job. Have fun, Dick.'

Sure, have fun. How, when you've just arrived and you're all on your own? I had another drink and began to think I should have taken Lady Donna up on her offer to tag along with them down to their stately home in Surrey. But I didn't fancy tangling with the English aristocracy on their home territory—too many guns and dogs and slavishly faithful retainers. There were other people I could have called, but the knock-backs had depressed me and I didn't want to risk any more.

The door opened and Simon Bentley walked in. I guess when you're an assistant manager doing a highly illegal favour for a guest you don't have to knock. Still, in my deflated state it irritated me. 'Afraid of bruising your knuckles, Simon?'

'Aren't we touchy? Price has gone down, Dick. Sorry. I think they're coming in from the Yanks in Germany. Supply and demand.' He produced a rather thin sheaf of notes and counted some off for me and some for himself. 'Plus my commission has gone up.'

'You're a bloody thief.'

'What's the matter, Dick? Some bit of fluff let you down? Sorry I'm not in that line of business.'

'You will be,' I said grimly, pocketing my share of the cash, which was considerably less than I'd hoped for. I was going to need to add quite substantially to that stake if I was to have any fun at all. 'Yes, a couple of things have fallen through. Where would a man go to play a game of chance these days?'

'I thought you were a member at the Bristol?'

I cleared my throat. 'Had a few problems last time.'

'The Peregrine?'

'Same thing.'

'I see. I'll have to tell the security boys to keep an eye on you. When were you planning on leaving—2 a.m. tomorrow, was it?'

PETER CORRIS

I laughed. 'It's not as bad as that. Come on, Simon. Somewhere to have a drink and make a few bob.'

'You could try the Double Ace in Tottenham Court Road. Any cabbie'll drop you there. Dress well and show your American passport and they'll probably let you in. Haven't got anything against blacks, have you?'

'No, why?'

'Place is full of 'em. I'm told it's the best place in London for jazz.'

'I've got something against jazz.'

'I don't think they play it in the part of the club you're looking for. Good luck, Dick. Have fun.'

If I was the superstitious sort I'd say there was something unlucky about being told to have fun twice within the space of an hour. After a nap and a tasteless meal in Oxford Street (food didn't improve in England until the Indian immigrants arrived when Britain went into the Common Market), I caught a cab to Tottenham Court Road. I could have walked it, of course, and would have preferred to as a way of settling the stodge, but the precise addresses of these places were the jealously guarded preserve of taxi drivers, who signalled their arrival with their horns the way Masons shake hands. I presented myself at the door—a solid-looking affair at the bottom of a set of ill-lit steps. I knocked and waited for a slot to open but the door swung in.

'Yes, sir?'

I recognised the doorman. He was Freddie Mills, who'd held the world light-heavyweight title a few years back. He was a full-blown heavyweight by now, full in the belly above his cummerbund, and jowly, but not someone you'd argue with at any length.

'Mr Mills,' I said. 'I saw you take the title from Gus Lesnevitch.'

'That a fact?' Mills growled. 'I KO'd him, right?'

'No. It was a points decision.'

6

The door opened a fraction of an inch more. 'Didja see the next one?'

I had. It was a vicious scrap at the Earls Court stadium in which a desperate Mills, mad as a Mallee bull,[3] had been KO'd by Joey Maxim in the tenth round. 'Maxim had the legs on you.'

'Maybe. So, who're you?'

I held up my passport and a five pound note. 'Just arrived in town, looking for a little action.'

I was wearing a dinner suit cut on the comfortable lines then fashionable. Mills looked me over like a fight trainer wondering if he could sweat a featherweight down to a bantam. 'No brass knucks, knives or guns.'

I let my arms lift slowly up from my sides. 'I couldn't agree more.'

He plucked the fiver from my fingers and gave me one beetle-browed nod. 'Welcome to the club, Mr Brown.'

That was close enough for me. I gave him a wink and slid past as he turned his attention to the people coming down the steps behind me. I read a newspaper article recently about something called 'passive smoking'. Apparently your lungs can be damaged by inhaling other people's smoke, even if you don't use the weed yourself. If that's true, every last man and woman in the Double Ace club was in grave danger. The air was blue, and the only thing to do to prevent yourself sucking in someone else's smoke was to light up a butt of your own. I did this as I pushed past the bare shoulders of the women and the padded shoulders of the men towards the bar. I bought a scotch and took a slow look around the room to size the place up.

First off, the ceiling was low, the space wasn't big and the noise was deafening. A black five-piece band that contained at least three saxophones was belting something out on a small stage. No point in talking about a tune—volume and beat appeared to be the only intentions, and they were achieving both. A few people were listening, swaying and snapping their fingers, but most of the crowd were intent on the usual things—spending money, getting drunk, telling jokes, and impressing the opposite sex. You don't find unattached females in places like this, but you usually find some that are detachable. I was looking for possible candidates and also for the door the serious gamblers used. Sometimes it's marked 'Private', sometimes it's not marked at all. I spotted it—concealed behind a big, bushy, potted palm. I bought another drink and was pushing through the press of hot bodies towards the plant when a hand descended heavily on my shoulder.

'Dick, old boy. Dick Browning. What the hell are you doing here?'

I turned, ready to fight if I had to or run if I could, as always, and found I was looking into the slightly bloodshot eyes of Peter Finch.

CHAPTER TWO

I hadn't seen Finch for a couple of years, but I'd followed his career in the trade papers. His original identity as William Mitchell, ill-educated product of a broken home, swagman, Sydney radio actor and artillery gunner, was a long way behind him. When I'd known him well in war-time Sydney,[4] he was clearly on his way up and out. Australian stage, radio and films had no hope of holding him. He had a big heart and a big talent and I'd felt then that, providing his mad drinking habits didn't kill him in his thirties, he could give the West End, Broadway or Hollywood a hell of a shake. By 1952 he was well on his way—a protégé of Larry Olivier, who had taken him up when he and Vivien Leigh toured Australia—doing well on the London stage and getting film parts.

'Peter,' I said. 'Good to see you again. You're looking well.' I was shaking his hand as I was saying this, but really doing my best to hold him up. He was close to paralytic drunk. I was also lying; he was looking a bit pouchy and pale, the result of too many long wet nights. I managed to steer us through the crowd and prop him against a wall. He fumbled out a cigarette and got it lit. That was one of the problems with Finch—no matter how drunk he was he could still perform. He could speak more or less clearly, light cigarettes and go on drinking. He was capable of more demand-ing physical acts as well, like fighting and, I am reliably informed, making love.

'Great to see another Aussie, Dick. Really marvellous. Place is full of pongos. Let me buy you a drink.'

Now Finch had knocked around in Australia for a fair while, but he was actually English-born, and after his time in front of radio mikes and on stage he sounded about as Australian as Winston Churchill. Still, like me, he'd been in the Australian army and had got blind drunk in Kings Cross and that qualified him to claim any kind of comradeship he wanted.

'Looks more like the Congo than pongo-land, Peter,' I said. 'Don't tell me you're here for this bloody awful music?'

Finch's actorly brow darkened briefly. I'd forgotten that he didn't like jokes about coloured people. He'd spent some time in India in his youth and later. In Australia he'd sometimes been sunburned so dark he'd been taken for an Aborigine. He claimed he knew about colour prejudice from the inside. It was lucky that I'd followed up with the remark about music. He was a fiend for opera, so I recovered a little ground there. 'It is terrible, isn't it? No, I'm here . . . damned if I know why I'm here. Bored, I suppose. What about you?'

I was ready for another drink but doubtful about how many more Finch could handle before he'd want to fight every man in the room. I said something about having just arrived and being short of cash and he produced a note and pointed to the bar. 'Make mine a double.'

I got the drinks—a regular scotch for myself and a weak, highly watered one for Peter. He took a long pull and didn't notice the difference. He also didn't bother to ask for the change, indicating that he was fairly flush. He looked it—good suit and shoes, expensive haircut and he'd had some pricey work done on his teeth. He also looked miserable.

'I'm told you can get a game of cards here,' I said. 'I was thinking to try my luck.'

'Fool if you do. Every game in the place's rigged.' Finch shouted this, it was the only way to converse above the saxophones. But just as he did so the music abruptly stopped as the musicians ended a piece and his bellow could be heard for a considerable distance in all directions. Freddie Mills pushed through the mob towards us. He wasn't tall but he was wide and that seemed suddenly to matter a lot more than height. 'I'll have to ask you gentlemen to leave,' he said. 'That kind of talk'll only start trouble. Come along now.'

A dangerous look came into Finch's red-rimmed eyes. 'Who the fuck are you?'

'He's Freddie Mills,' I hissed close to Finch's ear. 'Come on, mate. Time to go.'

'Freddie Mills?' Finch guffawed. 'Fainting Freddie? How many rounds did you last against Maxim? One, was it, or two?'

'Shut your stupid face!'

Hard to say who threw the first punch. Finch's wide, round-house swing missed and landed on a man standing close to Mills. Mills's straight right caught Peter on the chin and he sagged for a second, but alcohol had dulled all pain and he shoved the person he'd been thrown against away and swung again, hitting a woman. The man he'd hit, meantime, aimed a blow at me. I ducked and the guy behind me took the punch on the nose. Blood flowed. Then everyone was pushing and shoving and punching. Women screamed and glass broke. The band blasted a roar of sound but even that was drowned out by the shrieking and up-turning of chairs and the shouted curses and yelps of pain.

I'm an old hand at staying out of trouble in this sort of situation. I dropped to my hands and knees and began to crawl towards the door. Adopting this technique, and with a little luck, you can escape with a few bruises on your back and bum. Not so this time. I hadn't gone far before I was hauled to my feet by the biggest, blackest man I'd ever seen. He had a huge fistful of the back of my shirt and tuxedo jacket and he lifted me clear of the floor.

'Thought I heard you say somethin' about the Congo, man,' he shouted.

'A joke,' I bleated.

He smiled, showing gold-filled teeth but no humour. 'I figure to smash your white face in.'

Just then a tiny woman in a gold lamé dress rammed her hand into the black giant's crotch and took a grip of his privates. His eyes rolled back in either agony or ecstasy and he dropped me like a sack of coal. I scuttled away and found Finch, on all fours under a table, dabbing with a handkerchief at a young woman's swollen eye.

'I hit her,' he said. 'My god, I hit her. I've never hit a woman before.'

She looked ready to let him hit her again with whatever he could lay his hand on. Finch had that sort of effect on women. 'It was an accident,' she said. 'I quite understand. It's all right, really it is.'

Pretty soon, I judged, they'd be doing it, down there in the spilled drinks and cigarette butts. I moved past them but Peter hauled me back. 'Have to get her out of here,' he whispered. 'Have to sweeten her up. Can't afford to have any charges laid. Got my career to think of.'

He pushed her towards me and I had the choice of falling backwards and getting trampled or pulling her up and using her as a battering ram through the crowd. I chose the latter and, strangely, the bodies parted in front of us. It was then I realised that her dress had torn in the front, that my rough grab at her had pulled her brassiere down, and that it was her young, pointy tits I was thrusting at the mob. I was holding her just below them and she was shouting. No wonder everyone got out of the way. We were almost to the door when a man stepped in front of me.

'Charlie!' the distressed damsel yelled, 'Charlie, he attacked me!'

People were pouring past, bullocking their way up the stairs to the street, and the band was playing at full bore, as if the fighting had turned up the volume knob. I tried to shake free of the woman but she was clinging to my arm and still shouting to this Charlie character that I'd attacked her. That's when I made my big mistake. I broke her grip and aimed a punch at Charlie's nose. He blocked it, stepped aside and hit me in the belly. I bent double and when I looked up he was holding his warrant card close to my face.

'Chief Inspector Charles Partridge,' he shouted. 'You're under arrest for indecent assault.'

A senior Scotland Yard detective is about the last person you'd expect to meet in a place like the Double Ace, unless he's working on the quiet in some way, in which event you wouldn't expect him to start arresting people. But Partridge was one of your rare, but not unknown, playboy policemen—all Eton and Oxford and headed for the top. That night he'd simply been out for a good time with his girlfriend, and I gave him a chance to top the night off by showing her what sort of clout he really had.

Within seconds of Partridge's announcement the street seemed to be filled with uniformed cops and cars with wailing sirens. I was bundled into the back of a police van along with several other victims, all black, and we were off to the Charing Cross lock-up. I've been in police vans before and usually experienced some kind of camaraderie. Not this time. My three companions exchanged looks and nods and one produced a knife and held it to my throat while the others took my wallet and what little cash I had in my pockets. The one with the knife was an expert; if I'd spoken a word the movement would have drawn blood.

When they were satisfied they had everything worth taking, including my lighter, cigarettes, wristwatch and cufflinks, the switchblade was withdrawn.

'The mouth shut, man. Understand?'

I nodded as the van screeched to a stop. The door opened and a policeman tapped the nearest occupant on the knee with his truncheon.

'Out! Lively, now.'

I stumbled as I stepped out of the van and I fancy one of the negroes gave me a nudge. Anyway, I lost balance and fell forward, thumping my head on the pavement. I felt a boot touch my ribs, not hard, almost delicately, but so well-placed that it hurt.

'Get up, you. What're you doing down there?'

I scrambled up, very dazed, and shuffled forward along with the men who'd robbed me and threatened my life. I had a frightened impulse to laugh and must have done so because I felt a truncheon rap me painfully on the elbow. 'Nothing for you to laugh at here, sunshine. Nothing at all.'

We were shoved into the gloomy, damp-smelling booking section of the lock-up. The blacks gave their names and addresses and were marched off down a corridor. I stood with my back against a wall while three policemen conferred about what should be done with me. Eventually they agreed that I should be put in a holding cell until Partridge turned up with the details of the charge.

'Could be quite a while,' one of them sniggered. 'He probably has to tuck that bit of fluff up cosy first.'

'Lucky blighter. Right, you. Name?'

I opened my mouth but I couldn't find the right words. I gulped and swallowed and tried again. But I said nothing. I couldn't remember my own name or anything that had happened to me before my head had hit the bricks outside the nick. I blinked and shook my head, sending waves of pain surging through my skull. I sagged against the wall. 'I . . . I don't know.'

The sergeant closed the book he'd been about to make an entry in and sighed. 'That's your game, is it? Righto. Constable Lewis, pop him in a box.'

'I demand to see my solicitor.'

'How can a man who doesn't know his own bleeding name know who his bleeding solicitor is?'

My mind was totally fogged. 'I . . . yes, that's right. But I must have . . .' I slapped my pockets, feeling for my wallet, but discovered I was carrying no personal possessions.

The sergeant nodded to Constable Lewis, who grabbed my arm. 'You're not bad at it,' he said, 'I'll give you that. But from what I've seen it gets boring. And we're used to being bored. So we generally do better at the waiting game than geezers who pretend to have lost their memories.'

'Just a minute,' I pleaded. 'I'm not pretending. I fell over out there and hit my head . . .'

The sergeant grinned. 'Old one. Seen it a hundred and two times.'

'Please. Give me a minute. I'm sure it'll come back to me. It has to!'

'Hang on, Lewis. Give the gentleman a sec. Yes? We're waiting.'

My head was throbbing. I couldn't think. All I could do was listen to the drumbeat inside my cranium. 'No. Nothing.'

'Very good. First class. One of the best I've seen. Tell you what, I'll try you with a clue. Sure you're not an actor, squire?'

'I don't know.'

'Take him away, Lewis.'

I don't know how many gaols I've been in all over the world. Far too many. It's not a profitable way to spend your time unless you can write your memoirs or come up with a philosophy of life that will ensure you never get put inside again. These courses of action weren't possible for me then, even if I'd been disposed to try them, because instead of a memory I had a collection of fleeting and meaningless images and ideas that all seemed to contradict each other. I sat in the cell—the usual boring little box with a bench, a high ceiling and a slot in the door—and tried to remember. Trying to remember particular names, dates, tunes and so on is a thing we all do, some better than others. But trying to remember *everything* is quite different. When you think about it, it's quite impossible. I had no guidelines, nothing to hang on to. I looked myself over—six foot one, thirteen stone or so, some grey hair, obviously no spring chicken. I was wearing a dinner suit, somewhat dishevelled, silk socks, dress shoes. It looked as if I might have a bit of money somewhere, but I had not one penny in my pockets.

My head hurt. I knew why, but the only names I knew were Lewis and Charlie. Eventually I gave it up, took off my tie and jacket and stretched out on the skinny mattress on the hard bench. There was no pillow, an old trick to increase the level of discomfort, and I automatically bundled my jacket up and tucked it under my head. As soon as I'd done this I realised that I must have been in this situation before. Not a consoling thought. Still, I was tired and I had various aches and pains; I also had a fair bit of alcohol in my system, not that I was aware of this or could remember the pleasure of drinking it. I thought about chucking a shoe up to break the light globe, which must also have been something I'd done before, but I was asleep before I could do it.

Chief Inspector Partridge lost interest in prosecuting me, probably not wanting to draw attention to his own nocturnal activities. He came in to see me, wrinkling his aristocratic nose at the smell from my toilet bowl. I didn't have the faintest idea of who he was or what he was talking about, but he gave me a stern warning about keeping my hands off young women. I'd have liked to put my hands around his throat, but I had just enough sense to stare at him and keep quiet.

'Been like that since he came in, sir,' the sergeant, whose name I had learned was Barrett, said.

'Foxing.' Partridge extended his silver cigarette case to me. 'Smoke, do you?'

I shook my head. 'I don't know.'

Partridge smiled. 'He's good. Very good. Well, I'll leave it to you to arrange, sergeant.'

He snapped the cigarette case shut. Barrett looked as if he'd gladly have put Partridge's head in the stinking toilet, but he forced a subordinate's smile. 'Very good, sir.'

They got sick of me in the lock-up after Partridge cooled off and I suspect they only kept me around because they were worried I might turn out to be someone important who might make trouble for them because they'd treated me roughly. They gave me shaving tackle and the use of their bathroom, and I wore a police shirt for a day while mine was washed and ironed. I gathered that they'd made inquiries about me at the Double Ace and Freddie Mills had told them I had an American passport. 'Mr Brown' he'd called me, and that was no help to anyone. On the fourth morning I woke up and a name was in my head. I hammered on the door and the slot opened. Barrett looked at me through the grill.

'Well, well, it's the mystery man, making a nuisance of himself. What is it, squire?'

'Peter Finch,' I said. 'My name is Peter Finch.'

CHAPTER THREE

One thing led to another. Barrett got in touch with Finch, who took his time showing up at the nick. By the time he did, most of my memory—including the recollection of several incidents I'd rather have stayed forgotten—had come back. Despite the bad bits, it was a great relief to have the old backlog in place. There's something very frightening about it being a blank all the way back beyond the last time you had a piss. I remembered the blacks who'd robbed me, but they'd long since gone off to Brixton or the Scrubs and there was no redress to be had. I was let out of the cell and sat down to drink tea with Barrett (I hadn't yet remembered that I loathed the stuff), who concentrated on trying to talk me out of making a claim for unlawful detention.

'A lot of unnecessary bother, Mr Browning,' he said. 'And it wouldn't do you no good. There's not a mark on you, and Constables Lewis and Carney and my good self don't recall you falling down.'

'You don't recall the baton or the boot either, I suppose?'

'I don't know what you're talking about, sir. Best to forget about it really, now that our kind treatment has restored you to full health.'

'Jesus!'

'What's going on?' Finch appeared at the door, smartly suited. He sauntered in and stuck out his hand. 'Dick, old chap. Got down here as quick as I could.'

He sounded much more English than Australian and smelled only faintly of whisky. 'I've been here since the night we were in the bloody Double Ace,' I said. 'You might have made an inquiry.'

Finch's cigarette case came out and seemed almost to flick a Players into Barrett's eager fingers. He lit them both up with a gold lighter. I was still unsure whether I wanted to smoke or not. 'My dear chap,' Finch murmured, 'I inquired positively *everywhere*. There was no sign of you. I recalled you saying you were working on that bit of navy nonsense, so I checked with Rank. They'd heard nothing.'

Barrett flushed and he stubbed out the cigarette. 'I was in the navy. Would you mind explaining that remark, Mr Finch.'

'No offence, sergeant. I was in the Australian army myself and so was Mr Browning here. I was talking about a film being made. Mr Browning's an actor, you see.'

Barrett beamed. 'I suggested as much to him. Didn't I, Mr Browning? I thought you had a bit of the look of Sir Laurence Oliver himself.'

Finch glowered. 'Hasn't anyone in this country ever heard of any other bloody actor?'

I was puzzled by Finch's attitude but had no doubts about what Barrett was up to. I decided to turn the screw a bit. 'Have you got a solicitor on tap, Peter? I'm thinking of bringing an action for unlawful detention.'

Finch checked his watch and I saw the time. It was four in the afternoon and the pubs would be opening. 'Well, I suppose . . .'

Barrett coughed. 'Come on, Mr Browning. We're all old soldiers here. Surely . . .'

I was sick of Barrett's face and the sight and smell of his domain. Peter had his cigarette case out again and I took one, remembering suddenly that tobacco was my favourite vegetable. I recalled that I often fancied an afternoon drink as well. 'I'll let it drop,' I said. I gestured for Finch to light my cigarette. He did it, probably equally theatrically. 'I think you might owe me one, sergeant, as we say in Hollywood.'

'One what?'

'A favour.'

'Yes, sir,' Barrett said.

'I don't get it,' I said to Finch as we strolled towards St James where Peter said he had parked his car near one of his favourite pubs. He'd become quite the Londoner, Peter. 'I thought you and Larry Olivier were like that?'

Finch grunted and I gathered I wasn't going to learn any more on that subject. I asked him what the people at the Rank organisation had said, not that I was in much doubt.

Finch flicked his cigarette butt into the gutter and swerved to avoid a pram being pushed by an energetic young nanny. Being Peter, he gave the nanny a quick onceover before favouring her with a smile and a touch of the trilby. 'Job's gone I'm afraid. They waited as long as they could but finally had to put to sea without you. Bad luck, old son.'

I didn't blame them. Time and the movies wait for no man, except perhaps a *leading* man. As it turned out, *The Cruel Sea* wasn't such a hot movie and losing the job wasn't such a disaster as missing out on a part in *Gone With the Wind*. That was all Errol bloody Flynn's fault, of course.[5] God knows how far my career might have progressed if I'd been in *that* movie. As things stood, though, I had more than a few problems. I was in Britain with no passport, no money and no job. I'd recalled that my belongings were at the Regent Hotel, but they'd probably been impounded by now. I'd only booked in for a few days but I now had no way of paying the bill. I cast a sidelong glance at Finch, who was looking extremely prosperous. He caught the look and gave me one of his winning grins.

'Don't worry, Dick. I'm very grateful for what you did and for keeping quiet for so long. The riot at the club made the papers, but it's old news now and no one cares. I'll see you right, especially since it's partly my fault that you lost your job.'

Now all I had been going to do was try to tap him for a few quid, and if I hadn't lost my memory I'd have named him as a possible source of bail as quick as a whore can strip. But if he was in such a giving mood I saw no reason to object. I squared my jaw and marched briskly along with him. 'We colonials have to stick together, eh, Peter?'

He laughed. 'Even if I've become as British as Bulldog Drummond[6] and you sound pretty much like Gary Cooper with a touch of Errol Flynn.'

The light-hearted, approving mention of that name made me grit my teeth and determine to get from Finch everything I could. 'Look, I'm high and dry. I haven't even got the price of a drink.'

'I'll take care of that,' Finch said, and I saw that we were approaching the Guardsman's Gate, a pub frequented by actors and writers and other people who didn't have to work in the daytime. I had an Irishman's thirst after four dry days, but, while a skinful of booze would ease my pain, it wasn't going to solve my problems. I gripped Finch's shoulder as he was about to push open the door to the saloon bar.

'Peter,' I said, 'they were going to charge me with indecent assault of that girl you hit. Her boyfriend was a bloody copper.'

'Don't worry, Dick. Don't worry. I said I'd take care of you and I will. I'll square your bill at the . . . where is it again?'

'The Regent.'

'The Regent. That won't hurt too much. How does a spell in the country, a little London nightlife and a job on my next picture sound to you?'

Finch went past me and I followed him into the pub, thinking hard. *His next picture?* As far as I knew, the only thing he'd done in films recently was *The Wooden Horse,* where he'd played an RAAF officer in a role not so much bigger than my own. Still, he'd done plays in the West End, was close to Olivier and, as I knew to my cost, Hollywood had always panted after even semi-Englishmen—think of Howard and Harvey.[7] I was prepared to believe that Peter might be able to do me some good above and beyond a double scotch, although just then that was a pretty powerful inducement.

Thoughtfulness for the comfort of others wasn't normally Peter Finch's outstanding characteristic. Not that he was particularly selfish, it was just that he was used to people making a fuss over him and generally didn't have to put himself out for them. Men, I mean—he'd go to pretty extreme lengths of generosity for a woman. So when he came back from the bar with what looked like a treble scotch and a packet of Senior Service, all for yours truly, I could see that he was serious.

'Cheers.' I drank half of the solid slug and it was great to taste a good malt again. I lit up and looked Finch straight in the face. 'Okay, Peter, let's have it. I meet you pissed as a parrot in a lowlife club where you claw at the women and toss a punch at Freddie Mills. Freddie Mills, for Christ's sake! It has to be woman trouble. Wife trouble's the worst kind. Tamara's left you, is that it?'

Finch sucked down some scotch and shook his head gloomily. 'No, I could cope with that. I have before, probably will again. No, it's worse, much worse. More complicated.'

The pub was quiet after the afternoon shutdown and the drinkers were only just starting to drift in. We had a table to ourselves in a corner a fair distance from the bar with no one else in earshot. But Finch was almost whispering. He took one of my cigarettes, forgetting that he had a Caseful himself. 'You have to help me, Dick. For old times' sake and for what I can do for you now and in the future.'

I was getting impatient and finished the drink too fast. 'Look, Peter, you're sounding like one of the crappy films we play in. What . . .'

He noticed my glass was empty, tossed off his drink, jumped up and headed for the bar. If we went on at this pace, neither of us would know our own names by six o'clock. We must have looked a strange pair—Peter, very much the gent in his tweed suit, and me in my tuxedo, with my shirt gaping open, lacking tie, studs and cufflinks and very much in need of a bath. But the English will mind their own business right down to the gates of hell, and, besides, Peter was known there and, if I knew him, he'd probably been carried out at closing time more than once. He came back with the drinks and a couple of pork pies and some scotch egg on a plate.

'You look a bit peaky, Dick. Thought you might fancy a bite to eat.'

In fact I was ravenous—the food in the nick hadn't been good or plentiful and worry about my loss of memory had taken my appetite away. But I wasn't going to let up on Finch. I pushed the plate aside. 'Tell me what's going on, Peter, and no more bullshit.'

'I'm in love with Vivien,' he said.

'What?'

'Not what, who. God help me, I wish I'd never left Australia. I wish I was back in my monkey suit doing those bloody radio serials and plays.[8] I'm in love with Vivien Leigh, and I'm the most miserable bastard on earth.'

CHAPTER FOUR

In 1952 Olivier and Leigh were the biggest show business double act since Fairbanks and Pickford. She had won an Oscar for *Gone With the Wind* in 1939 and had just picked up another one the year before for *Streetcar Named Desire.* He had bowled them over in *Henry V* and *Hamlet* a few years back, collecting a couple of Oscars along the way, and he'd just finished *Carrie*, which everyone in Hollywood was saying was his best work in pictures. Of course, movies were more or less a sideline for him—he could fill any live theatre in the world for a year and was co-director with Ralph Richardson of the Old Vic. He could sing and dance; he could do any bloody thing, including pluck a young actor named Peter Finch out of Australian obscurity and launch him in London. I grabbed the drink and took a slug. I could see Peter's problem, but I couldn't see how I was supposed to help him with it.

'Have you . . . ?'

'Christ, no,' he groaned. 'That's part of the problem.'

'What problem?' I said. 'Just don't do it. Take cold showers, use professionals a couple of times a day if you have to, but just don't do it!'

'You don't understand. I'm insanely jealous.'

'Peter, you can't be jealous of a married woman. It doesn't make sense.'

Finch stopped looking sorry for himself and took on the steely look he was so good at. 'I didn't say it made any fucking sense, did I?

The marriage is over to all intents and purposes. Larry's more queer than straight anyway, and . . .'

'Is he?'

'Didn't you know? Noel Coward, Danny Kaye, all that sort of stuff. Apparently Larry and Vivien agreed to live as brother and sister, though a bit of incest goes on, I gather, especially when Vivien's tanked.'

'Which is pretty often I hear. But surely that gives you a clear run. Oh, I get it. If you start screwing her, he'll put your career down the john.'

'This is my big chance and I can't afford to blow it. But I meant it when I said I was jealous. I'm obsessed by her and I can't bear to think of anyone else . . .'

'Is there anyone else?'

'Perhaps not at the moment, but there will be.' Finch looked gloomily into his glass, and clearly not only because it was half empty. 'She can't help it. Men just naturally gather round her, wanting to do this, eager to give a hand with that. It's only a matter of time before someone fills in the void Larry's left.'

'Isn't she a bit older than you?'

'A couple of years. That's neither here nor there. Larry's flat out setting up LOP. I'm doing Mercutio in *Romeo and Juliet* at the Old Vic and . . .'

'You've lost me. LOP?'

'Laurence Olivier Productions. At the St James. He's an arrogant bastard under all that great man carry on. I need to finish the run and nail the film part. Then Vivien and I can take off together for a bit and see what happens. Larry'll understand, more or less, if we're working on a film together.'

'You're getting ahead of me again. *What* film, and what's all this got to do with me?'

I could see that Finch was nervous about spelling out what he wanted, and I wasn't sure how to play it. Basically, I didn't want to get up from that table without some substantial sum of money changing hands. I yawned impolitely and looked at my non-existent watch. 'Those bastards pinched my Bulliver,' I said. 'Look, Peter. I hate to ask, but what about twenty quid to get me square at the Regent? Then we could meet again for a meal and . . .'

'I can get you a soft job that'll pay you twenty quid a week and I'll double that,' Finch said abruptly. 'Plus, if things go right, a trip to Ceylon and a part in the film.'

This was confusing. I didn't know what bit to ask about first. 'Ceylon?'

'That's right. Ever been there?'

'No.'

'I have. The most beautiful country in the world, bar none. With the most beautiful women.'

'What job?'

'Chauffeuring for the Oliviers.'

'Jesus. What film?'

'It's called *Elephant Walk*. Vivien loves it, but Larry's not sure. I want you to encourage him to hate it.'

'As well as driving him about?'

'Exactly. And as well as keeping every other randy bastard out of Vivien's knickers.'

I didn't like the sound of it, but what choice did I have? I honestly thought about phoning my agent in LA collect and asking him for the fare back to the States or if there was any work going in England. That idea died suddenly—Bobby Silk wouldn't even have accepted the charges. I hemmed and hawed and we had a couple more drinks, but in the end I agreed. Larry Olivier had given Peter the job of finding a chauffeur acceptable to la Leigh—she didn't like fast or talkative drivers apparently, and Olivier himself was both.

'Larry mainly drives his own car,' Peter said. 'So you'll basically be working for Vivien. They've got a place at Thame, a bit out of Oxford. Know it?'

'I know Oxford,' I said. 'Got laid there once by a lady professor of philosophy.'

Peter grinned. 'What the hell did you talk about?'

Now that he'd got my agreement his mood had lifted and he was being witty. I didn't give him the satisfaction of a response. Instead, I extracted twenty pounds from him and agreed to present myself at the Oliviers' the following day. Peter forked over the money and scribbled down the directions on the back of an envelope.

'Notley Abbey,' I read. 'What kind of a joint is this?'

'Twelfth century. Very grand, which means bloody draughty and fucking damp until they spent a few thou on it. It's got a tennis court, a swimming pool and a croquet lawn. Pretty nice at this time of the year. Just two things, Dick.'

I finished what must have been my third or fourth solid scotch and wondered if I'd be able to handle things back at the Regent. The rustle of the fivers and tenners in my pocket convinced me that I could. 'Yes?'

'Hands off.'

'Goes without saying. I thought she was terrific in *Streetcar*, but you know me, Peter, I've got a weakness for blondes.'

'Your weakness for blondes is just a bit ahead of your weakness for redheads and brunettes and everything in between. Lay off.'

'Okay. What's the second thing?'

His grin was malicious now. 'I'm afraid you're going to have to wear a uniform, old son.'

At the Regent, as I'd suspected, they'd stuffed my belongings into my suitcase and deposited the lot in a cupboard, no doubt planning to sell it to cover the bill. I was able to do that and high hat them a bit, playing the eccentric American, something they believe in

quite as much as Americans believe in the eccentric Briton. I spent
the night in a cheap hotel near St Pancras and caught a morning
train towards Oxford. The month was September and the warm
spell, which had mercifully lasted while I was in the lock-up, was
coming to an end. As soon as we got clear of the suburbs the country
began to take on a wintry aspect, with bare trees and grass looking
as if it was flattening itself, getting ready for cold winds. It made me
yearn for California or Australia.

English trains were badly-ventilated and rattled a good deal,
the third-class carriages anyway, and that was how I was travelling
because I only had what was left of Peter's twenty quid to work with.
Someone had left a copy of the *Guardian* in the carriage and I looked
through it without much interest. Writers for the *Guardian* always
seemed to assume that you read the paper from cover to cover every
day and were fully abreast of everything the paper was interested in.
I wasn't. The Charing Cross nick's favourite rag was the *News of the
World,* much more to my taste. Still, even the *Guardian* had a bit
of interesting news and sports stuff: the American Vice-President
Dick Nixon had gone on television to say that his wife didn't own a
mink coat and that the only gift he had ever received was a spaniel
named Checkers. I could just hear them in Hollywood sniggering
over that. Marciano had KO'd Walcott to win the heavyweight title.
Bad news for me; I'd bet a hundred bucks on Walcott with Johnny
Stompanato, who bet on every *paisan* who knew how to get his hand
in a glove. Still, it was going to be another hard bet for the 'Stomp'
to collect on.[9]

Train travel in England is a very different proposition from train
travel in the States. There, you'll almost certainly get into conversation with someone, especially in the smoking compartment.

'Going far, buddy?' someone will ask, or they'll say 'Sure is
the way to travel', or 'Say, that's a pretty little town we just passed
through—reminds me of Forked Tongue, Minnesota'. Not so with
the English. The other passengers read their papers and books and

did their crosswords or stared mutely out the window and I did the same. I'm not sure what behaviour I prefer. All I know is that there's no happy medium between the two. I looked at the birches and elms and oaks or whatever the hell they were, saw them bending to a stiff and no doubt cold wind, and began to feel the need of a drink. There was a canteen on the train and I passed through several carriages to get to it. One good thing about the English manner in those days was that my luggage was safe in the rack above my seat. No one would have dreamed of stealing it.

After a couple of pints I began to feel better. English beer tastes like soapsuds until you get the second one down, and then you begin to like it. I sipped the third pint leaning against the swaying door jamb with a Senior Service going and the countryside unrolling. I had no passport, and no driving licence, for that matter, but such things could be attended to. Surely the Oliviers would be getting down to London a fair bit, and a chauffeur gets a considerable amount of time off. The money was certainly good if Finch kept his word. Everything found was the rule, so I might actually save some cash. Knowing actors, there was bound to be a maid or two on the premises and perhaps a nanny—I couldn't remember whether they had any children or not. I had my doubts about the trip to Ceylon and whether I could do anything to steer Olivier away from the film role and Finch into it, but I'd give it a shot. By the time the train reached Thame I'd decided that, all things considered, the prospects were good; I had four pints inside me and was feeling pretty chipper.

'Mr Brown?'

That name again, but this time it was being spoken by a rather pretty young woman standing beside a Rolls Silver Ghost. The car dwarfed her and she seemed to be trembling so much I didn't have the heart to correct her. I took off my hat and gave her one of Browning's reassuring grins. 'Are you with the Oliviers?'

'Yes, I am. I was sent to meet you and it's the very last time I drive this monster. God, I was in a blue fit every inch of the way.'

She held out the keys and her hand was shaking as if the gold ring and leather gizmo weighed as much as a house brick. I took the keys and gave her slender, green-gloved hand a squeeze. 'Richard's my name. What's yours?'

'Grace Drewe. I'm Miss Leigh's . . . dresser and . . . companion, I suppose you'd say. There was no one else to drive the car and I happened to let slip that I had a licence so she made me drive this beast, although I've scarcely driven at all. God, I'm rattling on . . . I was just so frightened! The lanes are so narrow, you see, and . . .'

'It's quite all right. You obviously did very well. As far as I can see there's not a scratch on it. Now hop in and you can show me the way.'

It was colder out here than in London and Grace Drewe was wearing a coat, making it difficult to assess her figure except in general terms, but she showed a very pleasing ankle and leg as she climbed into the big car. I put my bag in the boot and settled into the leather seat behind the wheel. Driving's one of my few genuine accomplishments and something I've always taken great pleasure in. To have the chance to drive this Rolls was a bonus and any lingering misgivings I might have had about the job (I still wasn't too keen on taking orders from actors or wearing a uniform) were quite swept away. I started her up and automatically raised my voice to speak above the engine noise.

'Grace, which . . .'

'There's no need to shout.'

And there wasn't. The car hardly made any noise at all. I slipped it into gear and moved off. 'Sorry. American cars are noisier. Which way do we turn?'

She gave me directions and slowly relaxed into the comfort of her seat. She'd been wound up tight, as any inexperienced driver suddenly put in charge of ten thousand pounds worth of car would be. She unbuttoned her coat and the promise of her shapely legs was fulfilled. The car handled perfectly and after a few gear changes and brakings I was familiar enough with it to drive it from Land's End to John O'Groats. I reached into my pocket for my cigarettes.

'You can't smoke in the car.'

A bit of a problem, that. I like to smoke while I'm driving, helps the concentration. '*She* doesn't smoke?'

'Oh, yes. *She* does but *you* mustn't.'

Return of misgivings. 'Difficult to work for, is she?'

'No,' she said flatly, and I realised that I had a lot to learn about the servant game.

Thame wasn't much more than a village, with a few shops and houses collected around a couple of churches and a square. We were soon past all that and bowling along down a lane with high hedges on one side and open fields on the other. The farms looked prosperous—solid fences, painted gates, sound roofs on the barns and houses, sure signs in the countryside that there's money coming in from somewhere else.

'Please don't go so fast. You never know what's around the corner. There are cyclists and hay trucks and all sorts of things.'

I wanted to get in her good books so I slowed down. 'Tell me what your job is.'

She chattered away for a while. I didn't take much of it in; it sounded as if she waited on la Leigh hand and foot from midday, when Leigh got up, to the early hours when she finished her last drink. 'I believe you got this job through Mr Finch? He's divine!'

I sighed and speeded up a bit. Another female smitten by Finch. I rather hoped that Lady Viv would be able to resist him—it'd make a pleasant change.

There were a few cyclists but no hay trucks and the only other vehicle in the lanes was a Morris Minor, which managed to squeeze past the Rolls by crowding up against a hedge. I really was enjoying driving the sort of car that everyone wanted to give the right of way to. I wondered if I might be able to make a bit of a splash with it—turn up at an audition, say, or a garden party. I was daydreaming along these lines when the lane joined a road. The corner was blind to my left.

'Turn right,' Grace said.

I slowed to make the turn and suddenly a big green car was coming at me on the right. It was moving fast and I could tell that the driver had seen me too late. *And* there was a van coming in the other direction. It's these situations that separate the real drivers from the wheel-turners and gear-changers. If I'd stopped, the speedster would have hit me amidships and probably collected the van as well. I changed down and trod on the gas and wrenched the wheel all in one motion. The Rolls surged foward and the car on the left missed me by inches; that put me in the path of the van; but I was already spinning away from it. I steered into the skid and let the Rolls slide until I had spun in almost a full circle, but clear of the van.

My hands were skaking and Grace was screaming when I trod on the brake. 'It's okay,' I said. 'Everything's okay.'

Everything had happened too quickly to allow me to think, but now it all slowed down. I climbed out of the car and lit a cigarette. I couldn't have gone another second without tobacco. Both other vehicles had stopped and their drivers were walking towards me. The guy from the van was closer. He wore overalls and a cap and his face was pale. He seemed to have trouble walking. He grabbed my hand.

'That were greatest driving I ever did see. Well done, lad. Well done.'

The other car, I now noticed, was a Rover. The driver wore a suit and he was mopping his face with a handkerchief. This stopped me from getting a good look at him until he was up close.

'You bloody nearly killed us all,' I said.

'Wouldn't quite say that,' he drawled. 'Are you all right, Grace?'

'Yes, Sir Laurence,' Grace said.

CHAPTER FIVE

Olivier wasn't a big man, say five nine, eleven stone—five inches shorter and a stone lighter than me—[10] but he looked bigger than that. He stood very straight and there was something about him that made you feel you were looking up at him rather than down or on a level. He was about ten years younger than me but you wouldn't have known it. I dyed my hair, watched my weight and could always pass for a much younger man. The van driver had called me 'lad', and he wasn't just being friendly. Olivier, on the other hand, was lined and wore glasses and a moustache that made him look older.[11]

'That's my car you're driving.'

I came very close to swinging a punch at him or calling him a stupid bastard, but I managed to control myself. I took a drag on the cigarette, dropped it and ground it out in the gravel at the side of the road.

'Well,' I said. 'No harm done.'

'This is Mr Brown, Sir Laurence. Mr Finch recommended him as a chauffeur.'

The van driver removed his cap to show proper deference to the titled actor. 'You couldn't have a better man for the job, sir, if I may say so. I never saw a better piece of driving.'

'Right.' Olivier slapped my shoulder harder than he needed to and shook hands with the van driver. 'Well, I have to get on. Duty calls. No harm done, as you say, Brown. You can tell Vivien I'll be back in a day or so, Grace. Cheerio.'

He spun on his heel and strode back to the Rover. The van driver replaced his cap. 'Blimey, I should have got his autograph. My missus'll never let me hear the end of it.'

'You're lucky you didn't end up plastered all over that Rover's front bumper,' I said.

'Richard,' Grace breathed, 'do you think I could please have a cigarette? This gentleman is right—you're a simply wonderful driver!'

Cigarettes all round, leaving me with only one in my packet, as Sir Laurence roared off down the road in his green Rover.

Notley Abbey was a stately pile, built of grey stone with leaded windows and all the other features of medieval architecture—traceries, capitals, spandrels and the like. I heard a lot of talk about them while I was there, but, to this day, I don't know what a spandrel is. It was set on more than seventy acres and had orchards and a three-bedroom caretaker's cottage. The abbey itself (I learned most of this from Grace's nervous chatter as we motored sedately along) comprised twenty-two rooms with three large living rooms, seven bedrooms, a huge dining hall and a staff wing. I had won Grace's admiration, no doubt about that, and Browning's law is—never hesitate to press home an advantage. I put my hand on her knee.

'Staff wing, eh? Is that where you're housed, Grade?'

A giggle. 'Yes.'

'So that's where I'll be, too.'

She removed my hand and guided it back to the steering wheel. 'No, Richard. I think the chauffeur's quarters are in the caretaker's house. Outside staff, you understand.'

Don't ever let anyone tell you the English class system was knocked about by the First World War and swept away by the Second. I was there, after both conflicts, and believe you me, it was alive and well in 1952.

We rounded a bend, turned in through an imposing set of stone gateposts, swept up the gravel drive and there it was—Notley Abbey, all tiles, turrets and tall trees. There was an imposing area of lawn out front and a certain amount of ivy growing up the walls. It looked big enough to house half a dozen families instead of just one bisexual actor, his dipsomaniac wife and a cluster of servants. I soon learned that the master loved the place as much as the mistress hated it, and that the abbey was a haven for freeloaders, past and present lovers, celebrities on the rise and decline, and schemers of all kinds. I, of course, was one of the schemers.

I dropped Grace off in the front courtyard where I met Mrs Witherspoon, the housekeeper, who directed me to take the car to the garage near the caretaker's cottage, get myself settled in and await further instructions. I complied. The cottage was in fair condition but looked as if it would be cold and draughty when winter settled in. Another good reason to cultivate Gracie. I put my bags in the one unoccupied bedroom and mooched around, inspecting the garage, tool and garden sheds and all the other paraphernalia needed to keep two tennis courts, a swimming pool, a croquet lawn and several acres of flowers, grass and shrubs in good nick.

I lit my last cigarette and smoked it, looking out across the fields to a church steeple in the far distance. I could see a few horses in a paddock, of considerably more interest to me than the steeple. We'd passed a pub on the side of the road about a mile from the entrance to the abbey and I was beginning to feel a late afternoon thirst, as well as an anxiety about running out of cigarettes, when I heard the telephone ringing inside the cottage. I hurried inside and snatched it up.

'Er, Brown, here.'

'This is Mrs Witherspoon, Brown. Could you bring the car to the front. Her Ladyship wants to go into Long Crendon.'

Suits me, I thought. I drove the Rolls back to the courtyard, parked near the steps and waited with my hand on the back door.

I hung around there in the rapidly cooling air for twenty minutes before the door opened and she came out.

Of course I'd seen Vivien Leigh in *Gone With the Wind* and other things, but nothing had prepared me for the sight of her in the flesh. She was tiny and impossibly fragile-looking, as if a strong wind would blow her away. She was wearing a short fur coat over a silk dress and her walk was slow and graceful. *Too* slow and graceful. I didn't have to smell her breath to know that she was very, very drunk.

'Brown, is it?'

'Er, yes, madam.'

'God, an American. Whatever could Peter be thinking of? S'pose you know on what side of the road we drive in this country?'

'Of course, madam.'

She swayed a little as she reached the bottom step and I moved forward instinctively to steady her. The look she gave me would have cut glass. 'Why aren't you wearing your uniform?'

'I've just arrived. I haven't . . . ah . . . been fitted for one, madam.'

She got to the car and placed one kid-gloved hand on the highly polished bonnet. I could see that the car was holding her up, but she made it look at if she was just admiring the gloss. She lifted her head and drew in a breath, tightening the skin under her pointed chin. She must have put her make-up on before she got sloshed because it was perfect, if laid on a bit heavily. She was naturally fair-skinned and hadn't tried to hide that, emphasising a smooth pallor that drew attention to her big green eyes and wickedly curving mouth. She was an exquisite-looking woman and I could understand why Finch had lost his head over her.

'Yes, I see,' she said. 'You *will* have to be fitted. The last driver was rather fat, and you're not, are you, Brown?'

'No, madam.'

She slid along the length of the car to the back door, which I flicked open. Everything works smoothly on a properly maintained

Rolls and this one had had tender loving care. I wondered why the last driver had left his post, but Lady V wasn't exactly the right person to ask. I climbed in and set off. I'd noticed the turnoff to Long Crendon on the way in and took it. No sound came from the back of the car; I adjusted the mirror, ostensibly to get better rear vision, but in fact to sneak a look at her. Her Ladyship was fast asleep with her mouth slightly open. She looked nicely settled, as well she might—for someone her size the back of a Rolls is quite big enough for a comfortable sleep.

Long Crendon was a typical quiet little Buckinghamshire village with a short, narrow main street, a church, a couple of pubs, a post office and the usual collection of basic shops. I couldn't see what attraction it would have for Vivien Leigh. My first problem was to wake her up. I drove past the church and braked more abruptly than I needed to outside the Chiltern Arms. She came awake with a slight snort. I stared straight ahead.

'Where are we?'

'Long Crendon, madam.'

'Ah, yes. I want to go to the church. I think you've passed it.'

That was a surprise. I made the turn and cruised up to the church. She rummaged in her bag and pulled out a sheet of notepaper. 'I'll be about half an hour. Here's a list of things I want you to buy in the village and here's some money.'

I jumped out, opened the door for her and she walked pretty steadily up the path between the headstones to the door of the church and went inside. She'd given me two ten pound notes, and on the list were a few items from the chemist and stationers and two bottles of gin. I did the errands pronto, getting some gin and a few packets of Senior Service for myself and leaving me with enough time in the Chiltern Arms for a smoke and a couple of scotches. I kept an eye on the church door from a window in the pub.

'Up at Notley?' the publican asked as he poured my second scotch.

'That's right.'

He nodded, a few of the other customers nodded and that's all they seemed to want to know about me. I was contemplating another cigarette when I saw the church door open. I bolted my drink and hurried out. She was shaking hands with a man in a dark suit and clerical collar. A gust of cold wind ruffled her immaculate dark hair and blew his grey wisps about. They exchanged angelic smiles and she came back down the path to the car. I opened the back door but she signalled for me to open the front passenger door. The clergyman lifted his hand and she waved back. Maybe she was showing him her Christian kindness to the lower orders by consenting to sit next to me. The smile stayed on her face as we moved off. I sneaked a look across at her—she looked ten years younger than before. Whatever had happened in the church had done her a power of good.

I'd used her money to buy my own comforts and wrapped her change in the original note. I passed it to her and she dropped it into her coat pocket without a glance. 'Thank you.' Her voice was precise and clipped now, but friendly. 'Tell me, how do you come to know Peter Finch?'

'Er, well, from here and there. I've done a bit of acting and . . .'

'So you're resting between roles, is that it?'

'You might say that, madam.'

'You're an excellent driver. Grace was telling me how you managed to stop my husband from killing himself and everyone else on the road at the time.'

'Grace was exaggerating.'

Her peal of laughter was one of the most thrilling sounds I'd ever heard. I almost lost control of the car. Her laugh seemed to trigger all my senses at once—I smelled her perfume for the first time, my hands sweated and I had to blink to keep my eyes from blurring. Then she touched me, just a light resting of her hand on my arm.

'Is something wrong?'

'No, madam. No, I'm a little tired, that's all, and not quite used to the car yet.'

'I see. It's a good car though?'

'It's a beautiful car, madam. The best I've ever driven.' I knew that what I really wanted to say was something like, *You're a beautiful woman. The most beautiful I've ever seen.* I clamped my jaw shut and stared straight ahead.

'Don't call me madam. It makes me feel so old. What else would you feel comfortable with?'

I thought of the Hollywood actresses and how they liked to go by their original names, no matter what their ages or how many times they'd been married. 'Miss Leigh,' I said.

Her laugh rang out again and, although I'd heard the quick intake of breath and was ready for it, the sound had almost the same effect on me as the first time. 'Miss Leigh. Yes, I like that. I like it very much. I simply *loathed* being Mrs anybody and Lady something isn't much better.'

'You could be Dame Vivien Leigh, I guess,' I said. 'But that sounds way too old for you, too.'

'Yes, it does.' She sighed. 'The men have the best of this world, there's no doubt about that. And *some* men have the best of both worlds.'

I had a pretty good idea of what she meant, but I didn't comment, just kept up my superb driving and the strong, silent manner while she chattered on about this and that, mentioning Finch a few times and letting slip that she *loathed* Notley. As far as I could tell, she either adored or loathed things, with nothing in between. The light was fading fast as we made it back to the abbey.

'I feel we can be friends,' she said, 'and I can't call you Brown. It's too ridiculous. What's your first name?'

I told her and she laughed again in the way that made my toes curl. 'I'll call you Rich. Then people won't think anything of it.

Thank you, Rich, for your help this afternoon. You can give the parcels to Mrs Witherspoon.'

I handed her out of the car. In the dimming light she was stunningly beautiful and it was all I could do to stop myself from doing and saying something outrageous. As it was, I gave her hand the slightest pressure before she favoured me with a smile and went up the steps. I watched every movement of her slender figure until she disappeared inside the house. As the door closed my first impulse was relief that I had the gin and cigarettes and my second was a corrosive mixture of envy and jealousy directed at Peter Finch.

CHAPTER SIX

The next few weeks were art intense mixture of pain and pleasure. Just to be near Vivien was almost enough to make me happy, to be unable to touch her was a misery. Olivier was seldom at Notley around then. He was working like a dog at the post-production stage of the film of *The Beggar's Opera,* which he'd put money into, hoping to make some more. Olivier played MacHeath, of course, and did all his own stunts and singing. At forty-five or so he was too old for the stunting and ripped a calf muscle while attempting a tricky jump. He had a pleasing light baritone (I heard him warbling in the garden a few times), but not up to the standard of the other singers in the cast. If you haven't ever seen the film and it comes on television some night, go out—it's a turkey.

People came to stay for weekends and overnight—the Richardsons, Noel Coward, Terence Rattigan, Peter Finch. Only with Finch was Vivien the least bit happy. In his company she walked around the estate, played croquet and tennis and generally had a good time. As far as I could tell, they were keeping it platonic, but there were plenty of touchings and sighings. This was confirmed by Grace Drewe, whose friend I became. My passion for Vivien had put thoughts of other liaisons out of my mind and Grace, it emerged, shared my feelings. As my cruder Hollywood friends would have put it, she was 'queer for Vivien'. Her position was more complicated than mine in that she also fancied Finch. It was a weird household.

When Finch was absent and other people were around, including her husband, Miss Leigh drank.

'What's this "Rich" stuff?' Finch asked me one afternoon. I'd driven the pair of them into Oxford, where Vivien wanted to do some shopping. Finch was a great reader and he'd dragged me into Blackwells bookshop to buy the collected poems of Dylan Thomas. (I heard him reading some of the stuff to Vivien later. It sounded all right but I couldn't make head nor tail of what it was *about*.)

I was glancing through the latest Agatha Christie, *Mrs McGinty's Dead*,[12] I think it was. 'Just a handle. A bit less stiff than calling me Brown all the time.'

'Brown?'

'That's the name they know me by. I've got no objections. I don't plan to put chauffeuring on my CV.'

'Won't be for long, Dick. Things are going swimmingly. She's wonderful, isn't she? And she's practically stopped drinking.'

That's all you know, I thought, but I just nodded and we left the bookshop to stroll along the Broad back to the car. 'When you say swimmingly, Peter, what exactly do you mean?'

'Larry hates the script of *Elephant Walk*. He calls it colonialist crap. The truth is, he's too old for the part of the husband. Vivien's pressing for me to get it and I think I'm a certainty. You can practically pack your bags, old son.'

That was good news but it meant I'd have to get myself a passport. I still hadn't bothered to get a driver's licence. The truth was, I spent most of my time day-dreaming about Vivien and dancing attendance on her and I'd let important things slip. I resolved to pull myself together and began by reminding Finch that he owed me several weeks' money. He forked it across happily. I hadn't done much to earn it, but he wasn't to know that. He was getting good notices as Mercutio; he was in love with a beautiful woman, and had prospects of a nice, safe affair with her. For someone like Peter, which is to say a romantic egomaniacal optimist, that all added up to happiness.

Someone said, 'Never go to bed with anyone who has more problems than you do.' Wise words, I think. That was one of the things that kept me from making a move on Vivien. Another was a kind of loyalty to Finch, at least as long as he was paying me and holding out the interesting prospect of the trip to Ceylon. Yet another was fear of Olivier. As I say, he wasn't at Notley much and when he was I kept out of his way. Danny Kaye and his wife visited a few times and you'd have had to be deaf, dumb and blind not to see that there was something between the men. They were forever showing off for each other and their tennis and croquet matches usually ended up with one of them draping his arm around the other's shoulders.

Well, some actors are like that whether they're faggots or not, and nobody paid them any attention. Vivien, though, seemed to get more and more miserable, and the unhappier she became the more she drank. She scarcely ate at all so her figure didn't change, but another year of this and she'd be needing her first face-lift. I thought her distress was due to Olivier's involvement with Kaye, but my indoors pal Grace Drewe put me wise.

'He's having an affair with Dorothy Tutin.'

'Who is? Finch?'

'No, silly. Sir Laurence. She's in the film. She plays Polly Peachum and she was hopeless until he taught her how to act. And now he's . . . Oh, Vivien's so upset, Richard.'

We were having a quiet smoke together, sheltered from the cold October wind by a greenhouse. 'How did she find out? He's always up in London and she's very seldom there. Was it the old mutual friend routine?'

'No, you won't believe it. The little slut—Dorothy's only twenty-two.'

'I'd believe anything about this bloody madhouse. Tell me.'

'Dorothy's mother rang Vivien up yesterday and do you know what she said? She said, "When are you going to divorce Sir Laurence so that my daughter can marry him?" Can you imagine it?'

'Jesus!'

'Isn't it *awful*? What a terrible woman! And it made her so unhappy I'm afraid she drank far too much and we had to get the doctor and . . .'

I gripped her arm. 'Is she all right?'

'Yes, don't worry. You love her as much as I do, don't you? And Peter Finch adores her and Sir Laurence treats her like this. It's too awful.'

I gave her another cigarette and we smoked in confused silence for a while. 'She's going to London tomorrow to see a doctor. You will look after her, won't you Richard?'

Vivien sat quietly in the back seat on the drive to London. I thought I heard her sobbing once but couldn't be sure. I delivered her to Harley Street.

'Thank you, Rich. I'll be a few hours, I fancy. You can go off and see one of your girlfriends.'

I would rather have stayed with her to hold her hand, but I simply checked my watch and nodded. 'I'll be here, Miss Leigh. It's not my business of course, but I trust you get good news.'

She smiled, showing her perfect white teeth. 'Yes, that would make a nice change.'

She went up the steps into one of those buildings housing a bunch of medicos who are all angling for knighthoods and making a hundred grand a year. I drove around to the American Embassy and the Rolls got me admission to the carpark. Nothing further had been said about the uniform at Notley, so I was wearing a dark suit and looking quite the prosperous Yank. I'd earlier written to Australia House and got a copy of my birth certificate. I had the required photographs and a statutory declaration from Finch testifying to my identity and I knew the number of my lost American passport because it was easy to remember: 1001001B. I'd always liked the feel of that number.

Business was slack in the passport office and my application for a replacement passport was dealt with promptly and went through smoothly. I gave the clerk the Notley address and he looked suitably impressed. I paid the fee and was told the document would be ready within two weeks. Getting a new California driver's licence would be trickier, but I gave them the details and they undertook to help me with it. Altogether quite a pleasant experience. I think someone must have passed the word that I'd arrived in a Rolls—nothing impresses Americans so much as a high status automobile.

I had a quick drink and a snack in a pub and headed back to Harley Street. I was early and had to circle the block a few times. Eventually I parked, smoked a cigarette (outside the car of course), and Vivien appeared. She walked quickly towards me and indicated that she would sit in the back. I could see that she was furiously angry and I didn't dare question her.

'Notley, Miss Leigh?'

'Of course,' she said. 'Bloody, bloody Notley.'

I moved off and before I'd turned the first corner I heard her opening the cocktail cupboard in the back of the car and getting herself a drink. The bottle tinkled against the glass a second time almost at once and then again before we were out of the heart of the city. At this rate she'd be well and truly sloshed by Ealing. I picked up speed a little, wanting to get her home as quickly as possible. I heard the bottle and glass sound again before too many more miles and began to indulge a fantasy of carrying her inside. I could imagine the delicious lightness of her. I'd have to take her up the stairs to her bedroom. Perhaps Grace wouldn't be around and there'd be no one else to help her . . .

'D'you know what that bloody quack had the nerve to say to me, Rich?'

PETER CORRIS

She was leaning forward and I could smell the whisky fumes. Usually, as I knew, she drank gin or vodka: if she wasn't accustomed to scotch it could hit her like a ten-pound sledge.

'No, Miss Leigh.'

'Course you don't, weren't there. How could you? Silly question. He said I should have a child and stop drinking. Have a child! How, I ask you? How?' She laughed, and this time there was nothing entrancing about the sound. It was like a sort of soprano gargle—high-pitched and desperate. I stepped on the gas and could hear her settling back in her seat again. I drove, worried about her, not fully concentrating on what I was doing. I was jerked back to attention by the sound of the police siren. I glanced at the speedometer and saw that it was touching seventy.

'Shit!' I eased off and moved over as the cop car pulled alongside and waved me to stop.

I brought the Rolls to a halt, set the brake and looked into the back seat. She was fast asleep, curled up in the corner like a kitten with her chinchilla coat wrapped around her.

'Out of the car please, sir.'

Two of them, one, older, with a stripe and one without. No guns of course, which was a relief. *This'll be all right,* I thought. *They're bound to know Lady Olivier.* I got out and stood on the side of the road.

'Licence please, sir?' The one with the stripe was doing the talking.

'Er . . . I'm afraid I haven't got one. That is, I've got an American licence but I've lost it. I've applied for a new one but . . .'

'You were doing seventy miles an hour, sir. Or thereabouts.'

'Well, my employer became ill and I was hurrying to get her home.'

'Take a look, Constable Clark. So it's not your car?'

No 'sir' now, you see. The old class system rearing its ugly head again.

'No, it belongs to . . .'

The constable came back and interrupted me. 'Woman in the back, Senior. Asleep. Strong smell of alcohol. Glass on the seat.'

The senior constable leaned towards me and sniffed my breath. 'Have you been drinking?'

'Couple of pints back in London, over an hour ago. Look, Senior Constable, I'm . . .'

He produced a notebook and a pencil. 'Yes, go on. Who are you?'

'My name's Brown, I mean Browning. I'm an American citizen and I work for . . .'

'Is it Brown or Browning?'

'Browning. And that's Lady . . .'

The two cops exchanged a quick look. 'Richard Browning?' the senior constable snapped.

'Yes.'

He put his pencil away, snapped his fingers and the constable produced a set of handcuffs like a magician conjuring up a rabbit. 'I have to inform you that you are under arrest,' he said.

CHAPTER SEVEN

'What's the charge?'

He clicked on the handcuffs. 'Attempted murder. I must warn you that anything you say may be taken down and used in evidence against you.'

'I'm hardly likely to say much standing here on the side of the road, am I? What I want to know is what do you propose to do about Miss Vivien Leigh, or Lady Olivier, as you might prefer to call her—the lady in the Rolls Royce?'

The young constable's jaw dropped. 'Vivien Leigh! I didn't recognise her, but I think he's right, Senior. What are we going to do?'

The senior constable was made of sterner stuff. 'I don't care if it's Princess Margaret herself. This man is accused of a serious crime and I'm taking him in. You can drive the car.'

'A Roller, Senior? You want me to drive a Roller?'

'I don't want you to, lad. I'm ordering you to. Where does the lady live?'

The last remark was addressed to me. I folded my arms. 'I'm not saying a word until I receive legal advice.'

'Your lack of cooperation is noted, Mr Browning. Clark, get on the blower and find out where Lady Olivier lives. Then . . .'

'Notley Abbey,' I said exasperatedly. 'Near Long Crendon. Look, this is a farce. I've never murdered anybody or attempted to murder anybody in my life. Well, not really. I'm sure this can easily be straightened out.'

'Happen it can. You'll be glad to accompany me to High Wycombe police station, then, where we can deal with the matter.'

'Why the hell not?' I said. 'This country gets crazier by the minute.'

'Noted. On your way, Clark. I'll send a car for you.'

I wasn't really too worried, although I never like dealing with the police for anything more serious than jaywalking. So far on this trip to England my only illegalities were a little smuggling, and driving while not in actual physical possession of a licence; but that hadn't stopped me being locked up once and now arrested. But attempted murder was absurd; there had to be some mistake.

I'd left the keys in the ignition and I stood by, under the watchful eye of the senior constable, while Clark started the Rolls Royce and drove tentatively off with a very drunk double Academy Award-winner in the back. It's a strange world.

Something about my demeanour must have discomfited the policeman, because he seemed wary of me on the drive into High Wycombe. I sat in the front seat. The handcuffs were a hindrance, but I managed to fish out and light a Senior Service. He didn't object, although he refused my offer of one.

'Nasty habit,' he said. 'I never could understand why people take it up.'

I decided it was time to start working on him. 'I couldn't agree more. Tried to quit but can't. Started during the war like a lot of blokes and, well, there you are.'

He sniffed. 'Well, you Yanks only came into it near the end, and I suppose you got your bloody smokes for free.'

'I'm talking about the first war, Senior. I was at the Somme with the Australians, and I don't think there was a man there that didn't smoke, except a few Holy Rollers. You got what comfort you could, believe me.'

He took his eyes off the road long enough to give me a hard look. 'You're not old enough.'

'I was a kid, it's true, but I was there—Ypres, Passchendaele. You'd have smoked and you'd have eaten roast rat like the rest of us and cried for your mother at night when the guns were going off. I suppose you were in the last show?'

'I was.'

'Me too, with the Canadians. Age up a few years for the first one, down a few for the second, bloody fool that I was.'[13]

I had him rattled now. I smoked and looked out the window as he drove. He was a big, beefy type, carrying beer fat and inclined to sweat. His radio beeped a few times and he made a mess of responding. It was getting to him—the notion of explaining how he'd stopped Sir Laurence Olivier's Rolls Royce with Vivien Leigh inside and arrested the chauffeur, who was an old soldier with a distinguished record in two world wars. It was time to turn the screws.

'I guess I can make a phone call from the police station? Get on to my solicitor?'

'Yes.'

'Fine. And you are Senior Constable . . . ?'

'Clancy.'

'Clancy. Okay. I'll buy you an Irish whisky when we've sorted all this out.'

'I don't drink whisky.'

I rubbed my hands together and chuckled, clinking the chain on the cuffs. 'I think you will after this, Mr Clancy. I think you will.'

If it had happened in LA the news would have been all over the papers the next day:

VIVIEN LEIGH DRUNK IN ROLLS ROYCE. CHAUFFEUR
ARRESTED FOR ATTEMPTED SLAYING.

Being England, there was nothing like that. All the muscle that was used, all the insults and threats that were thrown about, all the influence brought to bear and favours called in, remained unrevealed to the public. In fact, nothing appeared in the papers. Constable Clark didn't whisper anything to any journalist and neither did the copper who came out to Notley Abbey to pick him up; no one at the High Wycombe police station let anything slip and I doubt that Sir Laurence Olivier ever heard anything about it. Certainly, there's no mention of the incident in his autobiography or the various books on Vivien Leigh—I've checked. The only person to suffer was yours truly.

At the police station I was invited to explain how my passport came to be found in the garden of a house which had been burgled and the owner shot at and wounded.

Worrying, but not too hard to account for. 'It was stolen,' I said.

'Where, when and by whom?'

'By some negroes at the Charing Cross lock-up.' I gave the date as near as I could remember.

A Detective-Sergeant Harrington was asking the questions. He was a ferret-faced, balding type who seemed to have a grudge against the world, and particularly against men better favoured than himself. 'And what were you doing there?'

Tricky to explain but I did my best. I'm afraid it all came out a bit garbled—Peter Finch, Charlie Partridge, loss of memory. I could see Harrington didn't believe me and I became a bit desperate. 'Phone Sergeant Barrett at Charing Cross. He'll confirm what I'm saying.'

Harrington sent someone off to do this while he flipped through the pages of a notebook. I couldn't tell whether there was anything written on them or not. We were sitting in a small, airless room that smelled of disinfectant. Harrington had refused me permission to smoke and I was getting fidgety. 'Do you know a man named Simon Bentley?'

'I don't think so.'

'He knows you. He works at the Regent Hotel in Piccadilly.'

PETER CORRIS

'Sure. Yes, of course. Simon. I do know him.'

'Right. Now when you entered this country you gave the Regent as your intended address. Inquiries were made there and Mr Bentley made certain admissions.'

Jesus, I thought. *The cigarettes.*

I was never much of a poker-face and Harrington noted my reaction. 'I think you know what I'm talking about.'

'A few packets of Luckies,' I stuttered. 'It's accepted, it's normal.'

'It's not expected by Her Majesty's customs service, Mr Browning. Not accepted at all. Mr Bentley further states that you were absent from the hotel for four nights after checking in.'

'I've told you—that's when I was in the lock-up.'

'Dates don't match.'

'I'm not good on dates.'

'That's when the burglary and the shooting occurred.'

'Jesus Christ, I want a lawyer.'

'Profanity won't help, Mr Browning. Why don't you come clean? It'll go easier on you.'

Senior Constable Clancy entered the room with a smirk on his face. 'No record of a Browning held at the Charing Cross nick, sergeant.'

Harrington lifted one scraggy eyebrow as he looked at me. 'Well?'

Of course. They hadn't charged me. 'Did you speak to Barrett?' I said desperately.

'On forty-eight-hour sick leave.'

'Fucking Jesus.'

'That's enough from your filthy mouth!' Harrington slammed his fist on the table. 'Stop making up stories and tell us what happened.'

'Not a word until I speak to a lawyer. I want to make a phone call.'

Harrington poised a pen over his notebook. 'Who to?'

52

'Peter Finch at the Old Vic theatre.'

Clancy and Harrington exchanged uneasy looks.

'He'll be onstage in *Romeo and Juliet,*' I said. 'But I want to leave a message for him to get a lawyer down here as soon as possible. Until then, I don't say a thing. And you'd better think hard about the penalties for false arrest.'

Harrington leaned closer to me so that I could smell his cheap aftershave. 'Smuggling, driving without a licence while under the influence of alcohol and exceeding the speed limit are serious charges, old cock. I wouldn't be making threats if I was you.'

It was all bluff and counter-bluff, of course. I could tell I had them worried that the burglary and attempted murder charges wouldn't stick; on the other hand, I was worried about what they *did* have on me. I also faced the prospect of losing my job at Notley and the other inducements Finch had offered. I made the call to the theatre and left the message. Then it was off to a holding cell for the night. I was becoming an expert on British nicks—the hardness of the bunks, the smell of the toilets, the harshness of the lighting. At least they gave me a cup of what they called coffee and some fish and chips and allowed me to smoke. I had a narrow cell to myself, a wafer-thin pillow and two hard, scratchy blankets. An Irish drunk down the corridor started to sing and my blood ran cold. There's no sound more terrible on this earth than a drunken Irishman singing flat, but this one had a surprisingly good voice and a wide repertoire. I've spent many worse nights.

Finch sent an overweight, middle-aged lawyer named Dudley Mathers. He wore a fawn suit with a flower in his buttonhole, suede shoes and smelled of scent. The policeman who escorted him into the room where we were to discuss my problem could hardly conceal his mirth. 'I trust you gentlemen will be comfortable in here.'

Mathers gave him a winning smile. 'If we need anything, we'll know just who to ask.'

I sat, unshaven, crumpled and tieless across a table from his sartorial splendour. He produced and offered a gold case containing two rows of cigarettes. 'Turkish or Virginian?'

'Virginian, thanks.'

He took one of the other kind and lit us both up. 'No exotic tastes, Mr Browning?'

'Plenty,' I said. 'But I tend to forget about them when I'm in the nick.'

He shook his head. His full head of silvery hair scarcely moved but scent wafted. 'Bad mistake. Mustn't let them get the upper hand. Now, what can I do for you?'

I told him the story and he listened intently, scribbling in a tiny notebook with a Parker pen. 'This is outrageous,' he said when I'd finished. 'Poor Vivien, being driven around the countryside by Constable Plod. Larry would be furious! We mustn't let him hear about this. There'd be no end of a stink.'

'What about me?'

He glanced at his notes. 'You say this Sergeant Barrett will confirm your story?'

'Yes.'

'Good. I'll get on to him the minute he's back on duty. That should clear up the attempted murder nonsense.'

'That means another day and night in here for me,' I protested.

Mathers put his pen and notebook away in his tooled leather briefcase and heaved himself up. 'Best thing all round. Gives me time to talk to this Bentley chap at the Regent. That's your big worry, the smuggling business. See what I can do.'

'I thought you'd get me out now.'

'Don't be silly. They haven't formally charged you yet. If I pressed them now, they would. Then it'd be a full court hearing and a pretty penny you'd have to put up for bail. This way, all they'll have is the smuggling, maybe not even that, and the motor offences. We can see a magistrate tomorrow morning and have you out on a hundred quid recognisance. You have got a hundred quid, I suppose?'

'Sure.'

'Good. Leave everything to me. Twenty-four hours, Dicky. Cheerio.'

Back to the cell, running out of cigarettes, unable to drink the tea, unwilling to eat the food. Twenty-four hours passed and then another twenty-four. The drunk with the sweet tenor voice was released and replaced by a mumbling old sinner who hawked and spat all through the night. I was given a blunt razor, a cake of nasty-smelling soap and a thin towel and allowed a lukewarm shower. One of the coppers took pity on me and passed in a pack of cards. Well, almost a pack. It was missing the three of spades and the jack of hearts but I improvised with bits of the Senior Service packet and they helped to pass the time.

Forty-eight hours after Mathers had given me his guarantee he turned up again and I was let out of the cell. My watch, braces and shoelaces were returned to me and I was shown into a slightly more salubrious interviewing room than the one I'd been in initially. Mathers sat at a table while a distinctly uncomfortable-looking Detective-Sergeant Harrington stood by the window.

'Ah, here we are,' Mathers said.

'Yeah, I've been here all along but you're a day late.' I reached rudely for his cigarette case and took one, lighting it with my own lighter.

Mathers chuckled. 'Unavoidable, I'm afraid. But a happy outcome just the same.'

Harrington hadn't said a word. I sat down and put my wallet on the table. Not trusting the gardener at Notley, I'd taken to keeping my money on me. There were several hundred pounds in the wallet. 'How much is this going to cost me?'

'Not a thing,' Mathers said. 'All charges against you are dropped.'

You might think that the heart of a man in my position would leap up at these words, but I'd been around police and lawyers too much to feel any elation. Harrington was looking sour but not defeated. I drew on my cigarette and tapped off the ash. 'Yeah? What's the deal?'

Harrington's ferrety features arranged themselves into the best he could do in the way of a smile. 'The deal is, Mr Browning, that the charges will not be proceeded with on the condition that you leave Britain within seventy-two hours.'

CHAPTER EIGHT

In my time I've crossed borders illegally, fled countries and been arrested at air and sea ports, but this was the first time I'd been threatened with formal deportation. And me a former citizen of the British Empire, brought up to think of England as 'home' and the Crown as the untarnished symbol of just and fair government. Of course I'd found out while in the army and subsequently in Australia, Canada and England itself that this was hogwash, but nevertheless I was deeply offended. I looked at Mathers, who was wearing herringbone tweed today and a red bow tie.

'Are you going to let them get away with this?'

'Not much to be done, old boy. Got you dead to rights on the smuggling and the driving charges, I'm afraid. It's what you Americans call a trade-off, I understand.'

'I'm not an American. I'm an Australian, and I fought for this bloody country . . .'

'Can't understand a man giving up his nationality myself,' Harrington said. 'A sort of treason I'd call it. Certainly not something popular with most judges.'

Mathers adjusted the red handkerchief tucked into his right sleeve. 'You see how it is, Dick. Best thing all round is to . . .'

'Kiss ass?' I said.

Harrington smirked. 'No need to be offensive to Mr Mathers, Browning. He's done his best for you.'

'You can't deport me. I haven't got a passport.'

'Nobody said anything about deporting you. You're being . .
. invited to leave, and your passport is waiting for you at the front
desk.'

My resistance collapsed at that point. Looking through the window I could see a steel-grey English sky, threatening rain. The prospect of grabbing my passport and heading back to sunny California
was suddenly very appealing. I shrugged my shoulders. 'You win. I
suppose I have to sign something?'

'I've already signed it, dear boy. Let us collect your belongings
and go.'

I stood up and gave Harrington a hard look, but with a roughly
scraped chin and a wrinkled shirt and suit I suppose it didn't make
much of an impression. 'You've got a couple of West Indians running around breaking into houses and shooting at people, Detective-
Sergeant,' I said. 'I hope you run into them some dark night.'

Harrington's pasty face paled even further. He took a step
towards me and I was so angry I would have welcomed an attack,
especially as he was several inches shorter and a good deal lighter
than me. Mathers shoved his chair back and stood up.

'That's enough, Browning. Assault on a police officer would
land you in the Scrubs, and compared to that this place is a common
room.'

Harrington sneered, as angry as I was. 'Didn't go to a public
school myself,' he said. 'Perhaps you'd like to show me how things
are done there?'

'He would *not*! Browning!'

I allowed myself to be led from the room. Mathers soothed me
while my wallet, necktie and passport were returned. We left the
police station and tramped along the high street. Mathers strode
out, tapping the pavement with a furled umbrella. From the look of
the sky, he was going to have to open it at any moment.

'I need a drink,' I said.

'I couldn't agree more. Through here.'

We entered a pub, apparently known to Mathers because he steered me to the snug and was back with a pair of double scotches before I had taken two drags on a much-needed cigarette.

'Cheers.'

'You sold me out,' I said sulkily. 'What about false arrest, damage to reputation, loss of wages . . .'

Mathers sipped his drink. 'In a word, dear boy—cobblers. You apparently have no idea how savage this judicial system can be. Your middle name, I note, is Kelly and you have changed your nationality. Not something well understood in England as the good sergeant indicated. They could have tagged you as a dangerous IRA bomber quicker than you could turn around if they so chose.'

That pulled me up. I'd been in something like that position before.[14] 'Perhaps you're right,' I said grudgingly. 'But I can't get out of the country in seventy-two hours. There are arrangements, things to take care of . . .'

Mathers lit one of his Turkish cigarettes and gestured at the few quiet drinkers in the pub. 'Do you see anyone actually watching you now? Do you feel as if you are under surveillance?'

'Of course not.'

'Nor will you for, I should say, at least a month. Possibly more. Plenty of time to get your affairs in order. But they'll come looking sooner or later, you can be sure of that.'

'I wonder if I've still got a job?'

'My information is that Larry's been in London and knows nothing about this. Vivien has been ill. I'd say you'll be able to sneak back with no one the wiser.'

I didn't like his choice of words much, but, all things considered, I'd have to admit that I'd come out of the messy business in reasonable shape. 'Well, I'd better say thank you, Mr Mathers.'

'Dudley, dear boy. And don't bother thanking me if you don't feel like it. You could pay me instead.'

PETER CORRIS

The scotch and his campy cheerfulness made me feel better. I took out my wallet and the passport came out along with it. My California driver's licence was tucked inside.

'There you are,' Mathers said. 'All your ID, as you say over there. I must come to Hollywood one of these days. They do say there are some very interesting people to be encountered.'

'You'd find a few mates,' I growled. 'How much?'

'Let's say seventy-five pounds and I'll throw in another round of drinks.'

Mathers gave me a lift in his yellow MG sports car to the nearest railway station where I caught a train to Thame and then a taxi out to Notley Abbey. After all I'd been through I was relieved to see the ghastly place. I checked that the Rolls Royce was undamaged and then took a long, hot bath. After having a shave and climbing into some fresh clothes I went up to the house to get the latest from Grace. Mrs Witherspoon gave me a sour look as I entered the servants' wing but I ignored her. She had a right to be sour. Anyone with half an eye could see that the Oliviers' marriage, and therefore at least some of the servants' jobs, were hanging by a slender thread.

I knocked on Grace's door. She threw herself into my arms when she saw me and, just for a minute, I thought I might be in for a splendid homecoming, but she pulled away before things got too ardent. 'Where have you been, Richard?'

A chap doesn't like to make too much of things. 'Ran into a spot of bother with the law, Gracie. Nothing serious.'

'*I* heard you were arrested for drunk driving.'

'I hope that's not getting around. Quite untrue. I was the temporary victim of a gross miscarriage of justice. What's been happening around here?'

'Oh, it's been terrible. Quite terrible.'

'Vivien! She's not seriously ill, is she?'

'No, at least, I don't think so. But she and Sir Laurence had a dreadful row before you went off to London the other day. They're both in a frightful state and no one knows what's going to happen.'

Including me. 'Has Finch been around?'

'Yes, he's been ever so helpful.'

I'll bet he has, I thought. This was tailor-made for a seducer of his calibre, just like one of the situations in those dopey Renovation plays,[15] where Lord Prickleberry is screwing Lady Luscious while remaining the best of friends with Sir Simpleton Luscious, who is fucking Lady Prickleberry—you know the sort of thing I mean. Peter had the perfect opportunity to play the manly supporter of Sir Larry while insinuating himself ever more deeply into the regard of Lady Viv.

'I don't suppose he's here now?'

'No, but he phones every night. *She* won't take his calls. She's trying so hard to be . . .'

I patted her shoulder, and a very nice shoulder it was. I realised I couldn't go on like this. Another week of celibacy and I'd be starting to find Mrs Witherspoon attractive. 'When he rings tonight, fetch me. I need to talk to him.'

'What about?' Her jealousy was flaring in all directions.

'About the future.' I realised that she had moved back towards me and that her hand was on my arm. She was wearing a sort of silk sarong with a loose tie at the neck. From the look of it, undoing that tie might collapse the whole structure. 'I'm being deported, Grace,' I said in my most manly tones. 'It's quite unjust, but there it is. Other people are involved and I can't give you all the details, but . . .'

'Oh, Richard, you poor, poor thing. That's terrible. When do you have to go?'

'Few weeks, maybe sooner.'

She was pressed tight against me now, smelling like flowers with a touch of musk and unwashed silk sheets. I struggled to control myself. Always wary of women, my recent experiences had made me especially cautious. The last thing I needed was an accusation of rape. I needn't have worried; if there was any raping to be done she was going to do it. Her mouth fastened onto mine and threatened to draw the last breath from my body. She hugged me to her with a strength that had more to do with lust than muscle. My resistance gave way like a sluice-gate opening. I picked her up and carried her into the bedroom.

'Peter, oh, Peter,' she whispered. 'Yes, oh, oh, yes.'

I was past caring. She could have called for Larry, Vivien, Ralph and the whole company of the Old Vic for all I cared. I threw her onto the bed and we clawed off each other's clothes. I was right, the sarong fell away and she was wearing only panties underneath it. Who removed them I don't know—the whole thing was a mindless, frantic grapple with buttons popping and fabric tearing and hormones relaying their urgent messages. I entered her and she gripped me with thighs that must have been developed by horse-riding or hockey-playing or both.

'You're in,' she gasped. 'It's lovely. Stay there, please. Oh, please be slow.'

I was bursting, frantically trying to detach myself from the hot, sweet rush threatening to overwhelm me. I tried a trick a German whore had taught me. 'B iss der most boring lettter in zee language off Englische, ja? Bicycle, brick vall, Bonox. Zink off zose zinks, Richard, und hold on.' The image of a bicycle propped up against a brick wall with a sign advertising Bonox behind it helped me to stave off the orgasm until Grace had come in a series of short, trembling eruptions that shook her entire body. I followed her, bellowing, I'm afraid, until she clamped her hand over my mouth. She was lucky I didn't bite her, I was in such a state of ecstatic release.

'Be quiet, Richard. Shut up. Someone will hear.'

'Sorry,' I groaned. 'Got carried away. It's been so long, you see, and . . .'

She had rolled away and was rummaging in a drawer. She pulled out a sweater; a pair of slacks lay over the back of a chair and she dressed quickly. 'Yes. Well, it was very nice for me, too. And I'm sure it did us both a lot of good.'

'Gracie, I . . .'

She touched a finger to my lips. 'Not a word. We might even do it again some time. Now, what are you and Peter Finch going to do about all this?'

I stopped pulling on my pants and looking around for my shirt and stared at her. 'Do?'

'Yes. You don't think I'm stupid, do you? It's obvious that Mr Finch has some kind of a plan and that you're part of it. I want to know all about it.'

She was going too fast for me. I was still in a sexual daze. I shook my head. 'I don't know . . .'

Something very hard came into her tone. 'Do you want me to tell her that you've been under arrest and that you're going to be deported? Do you want me to tell *him?*'

'Of course not.'

'You'd rather we stayed . . . friends, wouldn't you?'

'Yes.'

'Tell me.'

I couldn't see the harm in it. I told her about Finch's angling for the part in *Elephant Walk* and his hopes for a tropical sojourn with Vivien. She laughed when I said I'd been supposed to put Olivier off the idea of being in the film himself.

'He hates it,' she said. 'It's one of the things they've been quarrelling about. One of the many things.'

'How sick is she? She won't be able to do the film at all if she's not well. Bloody hot place, Ceylon.'

She tidied her hair and straightened the bed. 'I'll make some tea.'

I was beginning to understand. I hadn't just answered a momentary need; she'd probably heard I was back and popped in her diaphragm right after slipping into the sarong. Women. Still, I had to admire her. She was looking after number one and that's what most of us are doing as best we can, and she certainly hadn't done me any harm.

'Haven't you got anything else to drink?'

'I've got some gin. I took it away from her room the other day. We've got to stop her drinking so much.'

'Gin's fine,' I said. So it was 'we' now, was it? Now it was my turn to wonder what her plans were. It was all becoming very confusing. She made two drinks and we both lit cigarettes. We weren't lovers and we weren't quite friends. I suppose we were conspirators, but it would have been hard to describe the object of the conspiracy. The phone rang and she answered it. 'Yes, I'll take it. Mr Finch, this is Grace Drewe. No, I'm afraid she isn't taking calls, but Richard Browning is here and he'd like to talk to you.'

CHAPTER NINE

There's almost nothing more frustrating and difficult than trying to have a three-party conversation on one telephone line. Everything Grace said to me I had to repeat to Finch and everything he said I had to relay to Grace. In addition, the line was poor and there was always the possibility that Vivien or someone else might pick up a phone somewhere in the house and listen in. In the end I managed to convey my problem to Finch as well as something of Grace's intentions. Essentially, she wanted to keep her position as Vivien's companion. She also wanted a part in the film.

'That's absurd,' Finch said. 'Has she ever done any acting?'

I conveyed this to Grace. 'That's not the point,' she said. 'I can get her well enough to go to Ceylon and work. I don't think there's anyone else who could. She's very close to a breakdown.'

'Bitch,' Finch said when I repeated this. 'But she's probably right. Okay. Agreed.'

I nodded to Grace. 'Can you swing that?' I asked Finch.

'I don't know, but tell her I can. Why should we put all our cards on the table for a manipulating slut like her?'

I didn't pass that on to Grace, nor to Peter my impression that Grace had designs on him as well as on Vivien. If we all made it to Ceylon there was sure to be some excitement. The only missing element would be Larry. Peter concluded with some words of solicitation about Vivien and I reminded him that I'd have to be out of the country in about a month and that I hoped he wouldn't let me down like Errol.

'Errol?' Finch said.

'You can rely on Errol Flynn,' I said. 'He'll always let you down.'

Finch laughed, said he'd stay in touch and hung up. David Niven somewhere or other delivers this line as if it was his own, but I swear I said it first. I'm not denying that Niven had plenty of experience—although not as much as me—of the bastardry of Flynn, but I still claim authorship. I suspect Peter repeated it to Niven some time and he slipped it into his book. Too late to ask poor Finchie now, of course, and Niven's much too grand these days for the likes of me.[16] I expect he'll be Sir David before he's finished, if he sucks up enough to the right people.

It was time to deal severely with Miss Drewe, sitting up in her sweater and slacks with obviously no intention of going a second round. 'You've got to get her off the drink. She has to eat and exercise. The last time I saw her she looked every day of forty-five.'

'That's a dreadful thing to say.'

'It's true. Finch is no spring chicken either, but they have to look roughly the same age in this picture, I assume.'

'You assume,' she flared. 'Haven't you read the script?'

I've always made a habit of not reading one word more of scripts than I have to—depressing and a waste of effort. I shook my head.

'Idiot. I've read it a dozen times. It's based on a simply fabulous novel by Robert Standish. I've read that, too. It's going to be a wonderful film and there's a nice little part for me in it as a nurse during the cholera outbreak.'

'How about me?'

'Hm, I'm not sure about that. She's got a couple of copies lying about. I'll get one for you.'

That was the big thing about Grace Drewe—in any exchange she always managed to get the upper hand. We left it there. All in all, I felt it hadn't been such a bad passage of play. (Funny how when in England the cricket language often seems appropriate, although it's not a game I've ever taken much interest in—too slow for someone of my impatient temperament and played with a bloody dangerously hard ball.) I was feeling relaxed after the sex and the solid gin. I could gladly have shuffled up for some more of both, but it was clear that Grace wasn't interested.

'You'd better make sure your precious Mr Finch keeps his end of the bargain,' she said. 'D'you think he can?'

I nodded. 'Regular operator, Peter. I'd trust him with my life.'

'Oh, don't give me any of that chaps-together *rubbish*!' she snapped. 'He's wonderful looking, of course, and he has that amazing voice, but does he have any brains?'

Implication: I do, you don't, who else has? A formidable woman, Grace, but not such a hard one to read.

I gave her a brotherly kiss on the cheek as I pulled on my jacket. 'You'd better hope he has, Gracie, he looks like being everyone's ticket out of this bloody mess. When's the genius of the modern English stage due back?'

'Tomorrow.'

I took a risk. 'You know he's got the hots for Finch, of course?'

'Don't be *disgusting*!'

As I said, a very complicated household.

Things returned to normal at Notley over the next few weeks, which is to say they returned to abnormal. Laurence Olivier and the Danny Kayes visited; Finch visited; Dorothy Tutin did not. I drove people around in various combinations and observed the steady improvement in Vivien's health, looks and behaviour. According to Grace, she had virtually stopped drinking.

'Just a little white wine with her meals and sometimes a drink or two at night after dinner to help her to sleep.'

'Good,' I said.

We were sitting in our usual meeting place out of the wind, having a cigarette and discussing the lives of our employers. It's one of the ways, I discovered, the servant class manages to remain sane. Pilfering, eavesdropping and watering the gin are a few of the others.

'What do you think of the script, Richard?'

Grace had got a copy of *Elephant Walk* to me and had badgered me until I finally got around to reading it. Somehow, reading has never appealed to me. I've always found other things to do when faced with the printed page, especially when faced with a great many printed pages. *Elephant Walk* was bulky for a shooting script because a good number of 'alternative scenes'—survivals from earlier drafts—were included in it, along with extensive notes on the psychology of the characters and the history of Ceylon. It wouldn't have been tolerated thirty years later when the time of a director and producer is measured in the thousands of dollars per minute. Nowadays, a final version of the script is a pared-to-the-bone thing that doesn't carry any signs of the pain that has gone into making it so skinny. I've known a good few scriptwriters in my time—Anita Loos, Dalton Trumbo, Ray Chandler, Hart Sallust, Ring Lardner Jr,[17] mostly drunks—and I know all about the third- and fourth-draft blues.

Briefly, the movie was about the brand-new, fucked-up marriage of a tea planter named John Wiley who takes his newly acquired wife, Ruth, from the suburban penny library she was running, back home to Ceylon. The huge house they call a bungalow is named 'Elephant Walk', and there's a vast plantation with scores of workers. Plenty of house servants, too. It looks as if Ruth has hit the jackpot. The trouble is that John Wiley is all hung up about his dead father—'the governor'—an old tyrant who ran a tight ship and is buried in the garden in a tomb. 'The governor' built the house right across a trail the jungle elephants had used since time began to get to the water. They still try to use it from time to time, but a high wall and shouting beaters keep them back. By government regulation, elephants cannot be killed. Wiley hates and fears the trunkers.

Wiley has a lot of friends who tend to stay for the weekend, getting pissed, playing billiards and a weird game of bicycle polo through the marble halls. Ruth doesn't take to any of this, particularly the worship of 'the governor'. The only civilised white man in sight is Dick Carver, Wiley's overseer, who seems to have read a book or two and can tinkle the ivories. Things then get interesting. Supposedly. I have to confess I only skimmed the thing and I was struggling to come up with a solid answer to Grace's question.

'Er, very interesting.'

'You ninny. You haven't even read it.'

'I've read enough to know there's nothing much in it for me.'

Her eyes opened wide in surprise. 'Why, I thought you'd be hoping to play the part of Carver. He's older than the Wileys and . . .'

'Yeah, sure. Well, we'll see.' I didn't need her to be going on about who was older than who and I knew I had no chance at all of the Carver part. Even with Leigh and Finch in it, they'd need a name actor for that role. An American too, unless I missed my guess. This was to be some kind of British-American co-production deal, and the folks in Boysie, Idaho, won't go unless there's at least one American name on the marquee. No need to tell little Gracie all that. She was such a schemer that it felt like necessary self-protection to keep as many things from her as possible.

I went back to the cottage to brood, drink and even have another look at the script. The story wasn't bad but it had its problems. There was something unlikely about the psychology of it. Do mature men still worry about their fathers? And even if they did, who'd care? I'd got away from my domineering old bastard as soon as I could and hadn't had any contact with him for thirty years.[18] It was odds on he was dead. Maybe Finch could make something of it. The woman's part was good; the Carver character was sketchy, but the sequence where the elephants break down the wall and reduce the bungalow to rubble promised to be exciting if they could bring it off. Well, there were various characters hanging around the house, planters, merchants and such. I fancy there was a policeman—could be another spell in *pukka* uniform for old Dick.[19]

CHAPTER TEN

The job at Notley became very boring. I was sick of driving the Rolls and polishing the damn thing, sick of the smell of its leather seats and the purr of its transmission. I'd gladly have swapped it for the Caddy I'd had back in LA, bad springs and all. Grace was cool and there wasn't any other female company about.

Vivien didn't go out. After Grace took her in hand she seemed to shed years and become more beautiful than ever. It was a slightly haggard beauty, of course, but none the worse for that. If she'd said the word . . . but I was merely 'Rich' the driver, always on call but not much called upon. I spent a lot of time just hanging about. I got pretty good at croquet, just from having not much else to do, and was occasionally invited to join the guests for a game. It gave me a chance to get my own back on them for their high and mighty ways. But being good at croquet isn't of much use and is nothing to boast about.

My month was almost up and I started to get anxious. I had a fair bit of money saved, enough to survive for a while in Hollywood while Bobby Silk tried to find me work. I guessed that the trouble there would have pretty much blown over by now.[20] But, like Grace, I was devoted to Vivien's interests as well as my own. I didn't want to leave her, even though my bounty from her table amounted to no more than an occasional touch on the arm or a smile. That's the sort of effect she had on people. Why Olivier looked elsewhere I don't know—unlikely case of familiarity breeding contempt, I guess. I was in this nervy state, two days short of the calendar month, when Finch phoned.

'It's all set,' he intoned in his most impressive voice.

'What is?'

'I've got the part.'

'Terrific, Peter. What about me and Grace? And do they know how fragile Vivien is?'

'So, it's "Vivien" is it?'

'Come on. I call her Miss Leigh to her face as you very well know. Answer the questions.'

'On Vivien's health, assurances have been given. I've secured a small part for Miss bloody Drewe, god damn her eyes, and I've got you on the production strength. Sorry, Dick, it's this American–British thing. The parts have to be farmed out according to a formula. But I did my best for you and there's one good aspect.'

'What's that?'

'You can leave for Ceylon in a couple of days. Your job is to scout locations, deal with local big-wigs, line up labourers, that sort of thing. You go on the payroll straight off, of course.'

What could I say? The quick departure was the right move and a few weeks swanning about in Ceylon on the production budget's money couldn't be too hard to take. I thanked Finch and told him I'd find a replacement driver locally.

'Thought you'd be pleased,' he said, obviously very pleased indeed with himself. 'This chap Andrews is playing Carver. Don't happen to know him, do you?'

'*Dana* Andrews?'

'That's right.'

Of course I knew him. Dana Andrews had been around Hollywood since the early forties. He'd been trained as a singer and a bookkeeper but what he really wanted to do was act. He was an enthusiastic drinker, and I'd got sauced with him a few times.

I don't know what his accountancy was like, but his singing was pretty good and he was a competent actor. 'Sure, I know him.'

'How old is he?'

Just like an actor, you see. Only worried about how he'll stack up against the rest of the cast. 'He'd have six or seven years on you. Looks it, too. He's a pretty fair drinker. Did you ever see *The Ox-Bow Incident?*'

'No. Sounds like a Western.'

'It is. Dana was very good in that. The movie got an Oscar nomination. He was in *The Best Years Of Our Lives,* too. I think that picked up four or five Oscars.' I was sticking it to him, you understand, knowing how he'd react to this sort of stuff. I was jealous and envious of him, I admit it.

'Has he won any himself?'

Even then, Peter was obsessed with winning things and, of course, it was the pursuit of the Oscar that finally did for him.[21] 'I don't think so.'

'Is he a pants man?'

'Not that I've heard.'

Like all competitive people, Finch liked to know as much as he could about the opposition. His natural confidence and optimism carried him on and he told me who to see in London about the job, where and when. 'When will the rest of the crew arrive in Ceylon?'

'December,' he said. 'We'll all be there for Christmas. It'll be great.'

I gave five days' notice to Vivien, who was having one of her vague days. She scarcely seemed to understand what I was saying and she just said, 'Thank you, Rich,' as if I was opening the car door for her. I didn't tell her I'd be seeing her again soon in exotic Ceylon. Although she looked better, she was still very pale and fragile, and she was going to need plenty of air conditioning, mosquito netting and parasols. When I told Grace that I'd soon be off she came up close and kissed me on the cheek.

'You've been very sweet, Richard.'

'Thanks, just what I like to hear from a woman.'

'Don't be like that. I was nice to you when you really needed some affection, don't forget. Now I want you to do something for me.'

'What?' I said, far from gallantly.

'Teach me to drive the Rolls Royce properly. I don't want some village idiot driving her about.'

'You mean you want to keep an eye on her, night and day. You're afraid she might drop in at the old Chiltern Arms.'

'It's for her own good. You will do it, won't you?'

I stipulated a fee and she agreed. One thing you have to say about Grace Drewe, she was as determined as she was capable. At first, she hated driving the big car but she set herself to mastering it. She had naturally good reflexes, excellent eyesight and a sound road sense, which is all it takes really. Once she'd overcome an understandable hesitancy about being in charge of a small fortune on wheels (my giving her the details about the insurance coverage helped), she handled the Roller with flair. I enjoyed the lessons, particularly the last one when I claimed my payment. The back seat of a Rolls Royce is a much bigger space than you'd imagine—quite big enough for a man and a woman to engage in an energetic bit of coupling. Grace and I parted as good friends, maybe even a bit better than that.

I had several hundred pounds in my possession when I caught a London train from Thame. This time I travelled first class and enjoyed the comfort—much more legroom, the aroma of quality cigars and a couple of very good brandies in the bar to ward off the chill. It was towards the end of October, and the English countryside is no place to be that late in the year. The further south you can put yourself the better, preferably somewhere with central heating, a few decent restaurants in the vicinity, and only a short dash to the tube, the pub and the off-licence. All that added up to Kensington, and I installed myself in Bailey's Hotel in Gloucester Road, near the station.

The movie production office was in Hammersmith. I caught a cab there and introduced myself to the bulky, middle-aged woman who seemed to be organising the show single-handedly at this point. Hannah Charles was her name and if efficiency wasn't her middle name it should have been. She had lists for me to consult, papers for me to sign, a cheque for me to deposit and my airline tickets to Colombo in two days' time.

'You'll be met by a Mr Da Silva who's already done a bit of the groundwork,' she said. 'You're to find locations for the scenes marked in this copy of the script and line up vehicles, support staff and caterers. It's all set out in the roneoed sheets you've got there.'

'Thank you.'

'Any questions, Mr Browning?'

'No, I don't think so.'

'Are your vaccinations all in order?'

I had no idea what was required but the first rule with someone like Hannah is, don't let on. I nodded manfully.

'Good. You can telephone or cable this office if necessary, but please keep any such communication to a minimum. I'd like a fortnightly report by airmail, please.'

'Sure. But the whole box and dice'll be out there in a couple of weeks.'

'There may be some delay.'

'Really, why?'

'That is my information. I'm not at liberty to say any more. Have a good trip, Mr Browning.'

Somewhat disconcerting, that last bit. I didn't fancy hanging around in the Colombo heat on what didn't seem like too generous a budget (the tickets were second class and the advance payment wasn't princely), while the stars got (as we would now say) their shit together. But that's the movie business—it's mostly waiting around for things to happen and praying that they turn out right. I dropped in at a travel agency, discovered that I needed typhoid and cholera shots for Ceylon, and took myself off to a doctor in the Old Brompton Road.

'National Health?' the receptionist asked.

'No.'

'Seventeen and sixpence, please. Fill in the form. Dr McMaster will see you soon.'

'Why do I have to fill in the form if I'm not on the National Health?'

'Don't be difficult, sir. Fill in the form. Next please.'

'The shingle says Dr McPhail.'

She ignored me. Out of annoyance, I filled in the form with a fictitious name, age, address and medical history. The only truthful thing I wrote was what I was there for. The wallpaper and carpet in the waiting room suggested that the premises had been a lodging house at one time. A fake chandelier and a tasselled velvet curtain perhaps indicated that it had done service as a knocking shop. The room was occupied by a pregnant woman, another woman with two mewing brats at whom the mother-to-be was looking uncertainly and an ancient gentleman with a hacking cough. I scooped up a couple of magazines and sat as far away from the cougher as I could. He had the look of someone who'd be happy to start up a conversation on any subject under the sun. To tell the truth, I've never felt comfortable about having needles stuck in my hide and I was feeling a trifle edgy. How people can do it for enjoyment I'll never understand.

As luck would have it, one of the mags was the *National Geographic* and it had an article on 'The people of Ceylon', suggesting that the original inhabitants, the Vedda, might be the ancestors of the Australian Aborigines.[22] As far as I could tell, Ceylon seemed a more pleasant place than most of Australia and I couldn't imagine why these Veddas would want to leave an island paradise for a place that is mostly desert. Still, it was only academic speculation and most probably wrong. There wasn't a lot of useful information in the article, but enough to suggest that the British planters who'd stayed on after the place became independent were having a hard time of it and that the Tamils, who'd done all the hard work for the past couple of hundred years, were looking to do a bit better for themselves.

'Mr Finch.'

I was deep in an article on 'The seaweed eaters of Yuzhuno' and didn't pay any attention when the receptionist called the name I'd put on the form.

'Mr Finch!'

'That's you, chum.' The phlegmy oldster who'd had his turn tapped me on the shoulder as he was leaving. Other eyes swung suspiciously towards me as I dropped the magazines and scrambled to my feet.

'Not much wrong with you, young feller,' a crone cackled. "Less it's your hearin'.'

I grinned to cover my confusion. 'Piles,' I said.

'Had 'em all me life. Winnie's got 'em. Why not us common folk?'

I was almost into the surgery before I realised she meant Winston Churchill. The British are quite impossible to understand. While all the paraphernalia in the surgery—equipment, textbooks, telephone, ashtrays—looked at least fifty years old, Dr McMaster was a young woman in stylish clothes and an expensive hair arrangement. She saw my surprise and smiled.

'Dr Ewen McPhail's my uncle.' She had an Oxbridge accent that set my teeth on edge. I'd have preferred a touch of the bonny banks and braes. God knows what the old hawker and spitter had made of her. 'I'm doing a locum for him.'

'Fine by me. As long as you're fast and painless with a hypodermic.'

She glanced at my form. 'I see, Mr Finch. So you're off (she pronounced it 'orf') to Ceylon?'

'That's right.'

'Will you be in villages and that sort of thing?'

'I imagine so.'

'You'll need protection against malaria. I'll give you some chloroquine. It's the latest thing.'

Old McPhail would have been a quinine man for sure, and my malaria protection has always been plenty of tonic in with the gin. But I've never minded getting the best and latest from quacks, as long as it doesn't hurt or cost too much. She scribbled on a prescription form and handed it across. Then she got up and busied herself with metal dishes and little bottles. This was the part I hadn't looked forward to.

'No chance of anything oral, I suppose.'

You couldn't make that sort of remark nowadays to a young woman, but things were different back then and she didn't even blink. 'I wouldn't have taken you for a coward, Mr Finch. Trousers down, please.'

I dropped 'em, yanked down the BVDs and leaned across the examination bench. The injections hurt like wasp stings and I suppose I flinched.

'Big baby,' she said. 'I thought you Australians were supposed to be brave.'

'Eh?'

'You're the actor, aren't you? You look a bit older in the flesh but I suppose that's the make-up. Pull your trousers up. It's all over now. You might feel a bit dizzy and sluggish in a while. Don't drive a car or operate any machinery for forty-eight hours, and whatever you do, don't take any alcohol.'

'And I was just about to ask you out for a drink.'

She smiled, showing big white teeth and pink, healthy gums. 'Your colonial charm won't work on me, Mr Finch. Try it on your wife.'

CHAPTER ELEVEN

Dr McMaster's parting sally depressed me more than a little. My marital affairs had always been pretty much of a moveable feast. My most recent wife, May Lin (I was never sure whether she was my second or third, the legality of my union with Carol Smith-Canneti being somewhat doubtful), had divorced me a couple of years back and I was sometimes acutely conscious that the only person who cared whether I lived or died was me. There was Bobby Silk, of course, but he was only interested in ten per cent of me, not the whole person.

I wandered back to Bailey's in the cold London afternoon, trying to cheer myself up with the thought of white beaches under the tropical sun—a bit hard when you've been threatened with malaria on top of cholera and typhoid. I collected my key at the desk and was heading for the lift when a tall, grey-haired man wearing a beautifully cut suit and a club tie approached me.

'Mr Richard Browning?' He had the accent of the British upper class overlaid with something else, a touch of army perhaps.

'That's right,' I said.

He stuck out his hand and we shook. The hand was hard in the way that only a hand that has done a lot of physical work gets. The strength of his grip contrasted oddly with the elegance of his clothes and made me look at him more closely. His skin was deeply tanned and the grey hair was premature; he couldn't have been much older than forty. His eyes were blue but deeply sunk; he was about the

same height as myself and I was suddenly aware that he was studying me as intently as I was him.

'Aubrey Pelham-Smith,' he said. 'I'm very glad to meet you.'

I don't like double-barrelled names, never have. I finished the
handshake, having tried to match him for firmness of grip. 'Mr
Smith,' I said. 'You have the advantage on me. You seem to know
who I am and I don't have the faintest idea of who you are.'

He laughed in a quiet, well-bred way. 'No reason you
should, but I hope we can be useful to each other. Can I buy you
a drink?'

There's no better way to get yourself acquainted with Dick
Browning. We went into the bar, which was quiet at that time of
day. I'd run out of cigarettes and accepted one of Pelham-Smith's
Players. He glanced at his watch, a no-nonsense affair on a leather
band. His hands were large as well as strong, and his wrist was thick,
almost freakishly over-developed. 'Half past four, near enough. I
generally have a gin sling about this time at home. I imagine they
can make it here. What's yours?'

'Scotch. Useful, you say. What does that mean?'

He gave the order and did not answer me, watching while the
barman made his drink. When it came he raised his glass briefly and
then sipped. 'Not bad. Not bad at all.'

I drank and it tasted like scotch. The thought crossed my mind
that Pelham-Smith might be part of what they now call 'the intelligence community'. Back then we just called them spies. I'd had
a bit to do with them, specifically the FBI and Australian Military
Intelligence. But I rejected the notion. He didn't have the look—
neither the arrogance of the top brass nor the furtiveness of the
lower ranks. But he had something on his mind, and the best thing
to do with someone in that state is to let him spill it in his own good
time, especially if he's buying the booze.

He took a solid belt of his drink and put the glass down, not
really interested in it. 'I own a tea plantation in Ceylon,' he said.

Bully for you, I thought. *I wish I did.* 'Is that so? Nice business to be in, I should think.'

'It was. My people have been in Ceylon ever since we kicked out the Dutch, in fact. The Pelham-Smiths did very nicely there for over a hundred years until I put a spanner in the works by marrying a Tamil. You know who the Tamils are, I suppose?'

I hadn't a couple of hours ago, but thanks to the article in the *National Geographic* I now had some idea—southern Indians, brought to the island to work on the plantations. I trotted this information out and Pelham-Smith nodded. 'That's right. Fine people, beautiful people, but very dark, and the Singhalese look down on them, of course.'

I'd had about enough geography for one day and was losing interest when Pelham-Smith tossed off his drink, ordered two more and said, 'How would you like to earn five thousand pounds?'

That got my attention. That was serious money, much more than I could expect to make from a few weeks work on the movie shoot. In general, the more money you have in your pockets in Los Angeles, the better chance you have of making more. Still, no one hands out that sort of dough for nothing. 'It depends,' I said. 'What would I have to do for it?'

Pelham-Smith smiled. His teeth were very white in his tanned face. 'I know you're going out to Ceylon soon. I've got a few contacts in the film business, you see.'

Oh ho, I thought. *You're looking to get your spread picked as a location.* That would bring in a few pounds, right enough, but not enough to cover a five grand bribe for yours truly. There was something interesting here, but the size of the fee was a bit of a worry. That kind of money smelled of danger. 'I'm off to Ceylon,' I said, 'you're right there. But I'm just a . . .'

'Production assistant. I know. But that's perfect for what I want. Look, I'll try to put it briefly. I got kicked out of Ceylon shortly after Independence because I was on the side of the Tamils. Made a lot of fuss, got into a spot of bother with the police. That sort of thing. Long and the short of it is that I had to hop it quick, leaving my wife and son behind.'

He spoke in a brusque tone, trying to keep all emotion out of it. But I could tell that he was finding it very difficult to maintain his composure. He lit another cigarette and his hand shook fractionally. 'My wife was killed a few weeks after I left. The boy got away and some people I know looked after him. He's nineteen years old now and causing the powers-that-be a good deal of trouble. Agitating and so on. But I want him here, with me. I want him to go to university, have a proper start in life. Then, if he wants to . . . well, you know. You can't stop young people doing what they want to do.'

'But what do you want *me* to do?'

'I want to get Ranu back home. You can give him a job on the film and then I'll find some way to smuggle him out. The government is enthusiastic about the motion picture business. It believes it will be good for the country's tourist trade. You film people will have a great deal of official support and latitude.'

I could scarcely believe my ears. Me, Dick Browning, risk my neck to spirit some wet-behind-the ears, half-breed radical out of a newly independent country that was probably overrun with trigger-happy soldiers? I was about to say no when Pelham-Smith whipped out a chequebook and began to write. 'I can't ask you to commit yourself, not here, not without knowing the lie of the land. But I'm willing to give you a thousand pounds now just to accept on a provisional basis. To look around and decide if you think it can be done.'

How could I refuse that? I nodded. He tore out the cheque and handed it across. I folded it and put it in my pocket. 'I was told you were a resourceful chap.'

It was time to do a bit of probing. 'Who told you that? Who do you know in the film business?'

We'd both finished our drinks and he signalled for another round, relaxing a little now that he was past what he probably saw as the hard part. 'One and the same, actually. Peter Finch. Family name's Mitchell, as you must know, and the Mitchells have Indian connections. I think Peter is by way of being a second cousin of mine, something like that.'

'And he suggested to you that I might take this on?'

'Yes. I met up with him at a polo game the other day. I knew about the family tie, you see, and I got talking to him . . .'

'Just a minute. If you've been kicked out of Ceylon, how do you manage to play polo and write thousand-pound cheques. Didn't they confiscate your estate?'

'Good lord, no. Nothing like that. They're not Communists, this lot. Just flexing their muscles and desperately down on the Tamils. No, I've got a manager in and he's doing splendidly. Revenues are up. But I can't enter the country and my boy can't leave, not without your help. I'm really most terribly grateful, Browning.'

'Richard,' I said. The scotch was getting to me but Pelham-Smith seemed unaffected by his three gin slings.

'Richard. When you get to Colombo go to the stall on the corner of the Street of Gold and the Street of Silver in the old town and ask for Mrs Tirrundrai. She will be able to tell you about Ranu and she can arrange communications between us.'

Finch, I thought. *Bloody Finch. Putting me right in it.* But what did I have to lose? The whole thing was probably unmanageable, almost certainly so by me. Perhaps I could talk to some embassy character in Ceylon and sort something out. 'I'll do what I can,' I said. 'But I can't promise anything. I haven't got any experience with this sort of thing.'

Pelham-Smith shook my hand and stood up. 'Nobody has, but I have to do something. I can't just sit around in this bloody awful climate doing nothing. If this doesn't work I'm going to go in myself.'

Like any old actor would, I slipped easily into the role. 'That doesn't sound wise. Let me see what I can do first. You never know, I might be lucky. Will the lad want to leave?'

He stood there, suddenly and for the first time, irresolute. 'I don't know. I just don't know.' He shook his thick grey hair and placed a card on the table in front of me. 'You can get in touch if you need to before you go,' he said gruffly. 'And I've written the name you need on the back of this. Tirrundrai, have you got the hang of it?'

I repeated the name. He nodded and strode out of the bar, looking neither to left nor right. Of one thing I was sure—he was sincere about what he had asked me to do. Either that, or as an actor he made Laurence Olivier look like a rank amateur.

I went up to my room, thinking to have a quiet nap before dinner. I planned to get on the phone and rustle up some company, possibly including a female or two. I was in funds, in work and with the prospect of some interesting times ahead. A thousand pounds to put in the bank. Things could have been much worse. I pulled off my shoes, slipped off my socks and lay down on the bed. I was about to close my eyes when I saw that Pelham-Smith's cheque had fallen onto the floor. I retrieved it and looked at it as pleasant pre-nap reading. It was drawn on the British & Foreign Bank, Colombo, Ceylon.

Clever bastard, I thought. *Well, just let anyone try to extract any tax from it.* I drifted off into sleep. Some time later I must have dragged the coverlet over me but I woke up shivering and with my teeth chattering violently. I burrowed under the blankets, desperately seeking warmth, although the room was heated and the air wasn't cold. Then I realised I was sweating even though I still felt cold. My throat was dry and my head ached. I got up to get a drink and my legs collapsed under me. I crawled back into bed and lay there, sweating, shivering and twitching with four-inch guns going off inside my head. I rolled over and my backside hurt where the needles had gone in. Then the plummy voice of Dr McMaster came back to me: *And whatever you do, don't take any alcohol!* Three double scotches. I moaned and thrashed, cursing all whisky distillers, Peter Finch and Aubrey Pelham-Smith.

CHAPTER TWELVE

My head was still aching and my knees were still weak when I got off the plane at Colombo airport four days later. Only a supreme effort of will had got me travelling at all. That plus a message from Dudley Mathers that a Home Office official had been in touch with him and had been gratified to learn of my imminent departure. I hadn't told Mathers about it. Finch again, no doubt. In those days you were only allowed to take a ridiculously small amount of hard currency out of England. I had a good deal more than the limit so I was nervous on the trip. My usual method of coping with nervousness is to take a little alcohol, but, of course, I couldn't bear the thought of it. The result was a very uncomfortable flight.

Moist, hot air wrapped itself around me as soon as I left the plane and the amazing thing is it made me feel a great deal better. God knows why. Perhaps I sweated the last of the unholy blend of vaccination and scotch out of my system. The combination of my height, obvious affluence (I'd managed to buy a smart cream linen suit before leaving), and the US passport got me smoothly through the entry system. The terminal was a modern building with tiers and decks something like a cruise ship in design. It was well maintained. I stood, fanning myself with a copy of *Time* and looking around for my contact.

A short, immensely fat man in a dirty white suit was holding up a piece of cardboard with the word 'BROWNE' printed on it. He was leaning back against a giant pot with a slightly wilted palm in it, smoking a cigar and looking unconcerned. No one else from the plane was paying him any attention so I crooked my finger at him—important to get off on the right foot in these situations, I always think. He saw my gesture, thought about it, took a drag on his cigar and sauntered over, rudely elbowing a few people aside.

'Are you Da Silva?' I said.

He gave off a strong smell of tobacco and various aromas I couldn't identify. He wore a Panama hat and was almost neckless, his third chin running right around and connecting his head to his broad shoulders. His black, bushy moustache either needed trimming or was on the way to becoming a full beard. 'I am Vasco Da Silva, yes.'

His accent was a mixture of English and something else, vaguely sing-song. His big teeth were stained bright yellow and I saw that the grubbiness of his shirt and jacket were entirely due to spilled cigar ash. I pointed to the sign he was now holding upside down. 'I'm Richard Browning.'

He looked at the sign as if he'd never seen it before. 'Brown-uh,' he said.

'No, Browning. From London, working for Paramount. You're here to meet me.'

He dropped the sign into a bin, threw his cigar stub after it and swept off his hat to reveal a head of thickly oiled hair. 'I am *honoured* to meet you, Mr Brown-uh.'

I shook the hand he offered and took what I've always thought of as the Australian option. When in doubt, keep it casual. I couldn't go through the next few months being called 'Brown-uh'. 'Call me Dick,' I said.

'Splendid! Splendid, Dick! Vasco.'

So Dick and Vasco went off to collect Dick's luggage which didn't amount to much—just the much-travelled bag I'd arrived with at Tilbury. It all seemed a lot longer ago than it really was. I had the canvas hold-all I'd taken onto the plane with a change of socks and shaving kit inside. I also had a bag containing two duty free bottles of scotch—I didn't expect my teetotal condition to be permanent. Vasco chattered the whole time as we walked to another building to collect the baggage but I didn't take in much of what he said. I hadn't been smoking lately either, and with all my senses alert I was picking up all kinds of exotic smells once outside the big shed.

The few glances I'd had of the coastline through the plane window on the way in had been satisfying enough—blue water, white sands and jungle, your standard tropical island—but what I saw now was really confusing. A cobalt sky with fluffy white clouds, low, dark green hills in the distance and flat, swampy country all around. A high, bright sun was casting the darkest shadows I'd ever seen in my life but, although the air was moist and hot, it was a pleasant kind of heat and moisture. I can't explain it, but the air of Ceylon had something special to it—perhaps it was just the contrast with the English late autumn.

We collected the bag and Da Silva insisted on carrying it. We seemed to be out in the Everglades, more water than land in sight. I lit a tentative cigarette, inhaling shallowly. It tasted fine. 'Where's the city?' I asked.

'Twenty-five miles south. I have a car.' He smiled. 'That is to say, the film company has a car and I have the honour to drive it.'

'And we're going where?'

'To my humble house where you can rest and refresh yourself. Tomorrow we can set off for Kandy and I can show you some places that will interest you.'

I thought of my cheque. 'I'll need a day in Colombo first. Bit of banking business and such.'

'Of course. Very sorry to rush you. Of course, there is no hurry.'

We reached an unfenced, bituminised space where cars, motorcycles, trishaws, pushbikes and wagons were parked higgledy-piggledy. Da Silva steered me towards an ex-army jeep that looked as if it had done service in the Solomons, New Guinea, Thailand and Burma. There wasn't a smooth piece of metal on it; the spare wheel was fastened on with wire and a strip of duct tape ran across a crack in the passenger side windscreen. Against that, it had brand new tyres with a ton of tread on them.

Da Silva heaved my bag into the back seat. 'A fine vehicle,' he said. 'Just right for some of the rough roads we will be travelling.'

I resolved there and then to travel as few rough roads as possible. Da Silva waved away a few raggedy kids who'd clustered around the jeep and started the engine. The last car I'd sat in the front seat of had been Olivier's Roller and the contrast was shocking. The jeep's motor clattered like an egg-beater and when he swung the steering wheel it shrieked like a cat being tortured. I felt the return of my headache and pulled out sunglasses from my hold-all. Da Silva released the handbrake, allowing it to ratchet back slowly.

'Noisy, but a most wonderful motor,' Da Silva shouted.

I nodded and leaned back in the rock-hard seat. Surely the budget would run to a better crate than this? I wondered if Da Silva was skimming already. I didn't give a damn unless it subjected me to discomfort. I began to worry about the amenities in his humble home. Maybe I should insist on going to a hotel.

We were haring along a narrow, rough macadam strip with a stream of other cars, taxis and a couple of buses. The motor traffic terrorised the horse-drawn, which fought back by deliberately going slow, especially around the bends. The jeep bounced over potholes and skidded in muddy puddles. I managed to take my eyes off the road to see how Da Silva was handling it. I nearly grabbed the wheel: he was ducking his head to light a cigar, steering with his knees and looking down towards his feet. I forgot about the hotel. Just arriving *anywhere* in one piece was the first problem.

I've never understood tourists. After a short time, I've seen all the paddy fields, coconut trees and donkey wagons I need, and a very few temples and shrines go an extremely long way with me. You've seen one display garden, laid out in the eighteenth century by the Governor's wife, and you've seen them all, and tropical marketplaces are hot, dirty, smelly and filled with thieves the world over. Da Silva pointed out the sights to me as he drove—the fortress, Cargill's emporium, the Pettah, or old town, this Hindu temple, that Buddhist shrine, this mosque, that cathedral.

'The black people are Tamils, the brown are Singhalese. I myself am of Portuguese descent with some Singhalese and Arab and German. I am a true citizen of this island.'

The streets of Colombo were crowded with hurrying people of all skin shades. Generally speaking, the darkest were bent double under heavy loads and the lightest were stepping in and out of trishaws and taxis. It's the way of the world. There seemed to be vast throngs of children in the streets, attending small stalls, selling tickets for God knows what, playing in the gutters, minding children younger than themselves.

I saw the British and Foreign Bank, a white edifice with an imposing set of colonnades, marble steps and brightly polished brass handrails. 'Busy place,' I said while we were stopped, waiting for a traffic cop to unsort the tangle at a three-ways.

'But very poor. We need very much outside investment.'

That's what everyone needs, I thought. Da Silva moved off and the motor noise made a reply impracticable. I just nodded drowsily. All I wanted was a long, cool drink and a sleep.

I got both at Da Silva's bungalow in a suburb on the south-eastern fringe of the city. The house accommodated a lot of children and quite a few adults. I never quite sorted out who was who, but Da Silva's word was law. He introduced me to his wife, a matronly woman who kept her eyes lowered as she served us glasses of cordial. Da Silva had only to raise his voice once for a silence to settle throughout the place. I was too tired to care about the disruption I was causing. He showed me to a small room with a mat on the floor and a narrow, low bed. With pride he switched on the ceiling fan.

'This will cool you,' he said. 'After you sleep we men will go out to eat and talk. I will drive you to your appointments tomorrow and we will leave at first light the next day.'

Bossy type, I thought, but then I had the feeling that a trip up country would be welcome to him. Maybe he couldn't get any peace and quiet unless he had a visitor.

As I crawled between the stiffly starched sheets I had a sudden surge of panic. I hadn't asked for any identification and here I was, with a possible imposter, stuck in a house, maybe under lock and key. I scrambled out of bed and checked the door. It was unlocked and I told myself I was being foolish. Still, I took my wallet out and put it under my pillow. In it was a fair amount of money, Pelham-Smith's cheque and the name of my contact—Mrs Tirrundrai in the old town. I was asleep under the slowly turning fan before I could give his domestic arrangements and my commitments any further consideration.

That night Vasco Da Silva and I went out and ate curry and drank beer in a small, smoky backstreet restaurant where you sat on the floor. After my few days of abstemiousness the food and drink were wonderful. Da Silva admired my ability to eat the hottest of the curries.

'Most Europeans can't do that.'

'I've been around,' I said. 'I spent some time with a mercenary army in Mexico. They eat pretty hot food down there—dog and lizard and such.[23] Doesn't taste nearly as good. I held up a piece of meat in a fold of *chapatti.* What is this?'

'Monkey.'

I switched to the vegetable dishes. The beer was a thin, sweetish local brew that I drank sparingly without ill-effect. Da Silva filled me in on what he'd been doing to further the art of the cinema.

It turned out that he ran a couple of small movie houses and had dabbled in production himself with no great success. But it had put him in touch with some of the bigger players and got him the job of scouting locations and otherwise troubleshooting for overseas producers. He named a few films—two Indian and one French—that he'd had a hand in. I hadn't heard of them but that didn't mean much—I spent practically no time looking at Indian and French movies. Anyway, it seemed that he knew his business and I was beginning to have confidence in him, up to a point.

'I'm not travelling in that jeep,' I said.

'I do not understand, Dick.'

'Tomorrow, while I'm conducting my business, you will find a better vehicle.'

'The roads are rough . . .'

I shook my head. 'Then they are the wrong roads. Vivien Leigh isn't going to travel on bush tracks. You're going to have to rethink it, Vasco. Better roads and better car. Okay?'

'It will cost more money.'

'That's not your problem. How much have you spent so far?'

He shrugged and ate some curried monkey. 'I have spent very little.'

'You haven't got the idea, my friend. Tomorrow we'll start spending it.'

The children woke me up in the morning by running around the outside of the house, also under it and over the roof, shouting at each other. I'd slept well and was almost amused. Mrs Da Silva, who must have known every inch of the floor of her house intimately from the way she kept her eyes lowered, made us a breakfast of fruit, rice cakes and tea. I drank only as much tea as I needed to wash down a chloroquine tablet. Then we got into the jeep and jolted our way into the city. Da Silva waited while I opened an account in the bank and deposited Pelham-Smith's cheque. I couldn't draw on the funds for a few days, but I changed some English money into rupees and walked out with well-filled pockets. It was hot already and I took off my jacket. I was glad of the Panama and the sunglasses.

'Where to now, Dick?' Da Silva asked.

'I want to go to the Street of Gold, it's in the old town.'

Da Silva's dark face, shiny with sweat and still covered with dark bristles, seemed to go pale. 'Where did you say?'

'The Street of Gold. It's . . .'

Da Silva waved angrily at a small boy who was touching the jeep's headlights. 'I know where it is. It's in the Pettah. But I cannot take you there. I will not do it. No, definitely not!'

CHAPTER THIRTEEN

It was time to put my foot down. I couldn't let him give me orders and deny me things, not if I wanted to run the show my way. 'Look, Vasco,' I said. 'I'm the boss here. Have you got that? I say what happens and what doesn't happen. Now you drop me by the entrance to the Pettah and take yourself off to find a better vehicle. Meet me in, let's say, two hours, and I'll come and have a look at your selection.'

Sulkily, he started the motor and drove off in the direction of the old town. The previous day I'd noticed a collection of maps and brochures in a compartment under the jeep's dashboard. Maybe Vasco was doubling as a tour guide, using the company car. I found a map of the Pettah and studied it as we drove. The map was a crude, badly printed affair, but the Street of Gold was clearly marked and I didn't think I'd have too much trouble finding it. Vasco stared straight ahead, sucking on a dead cigar and driving with more care than usual. He was clearly worried and his concern communicated itself to me. He pulled up in a square where hordes of people were pouring in and out of the narrow street that led to the Pettah. I offered him a cigarette and lit him up.

'Sorry if I was a bit rough. What's on your mind?'

'The place where you are intending to go is dangerous. I feel responsible for you.'

'I can look after myself. Why is it dangerous?'

'It's full of Tamils. They are a difficult, unhappy people, especially at the moment.'

'Yeah? Why's that?'

'The police have just shot one of their leaders. A saboteur. Things are very touchy.'

I paused, considering putting off my visit to Mrs Tirrundrai. But we were heading for the hills tomorrow, and it was important that I didn't look indecisive to Da Silva. I jumped out of the jeep. 'There's someone I have to see. I'll just be in and out. Meet me in that cafe over there. I'll buy you a beer.'

He nodded unhappily and drove off. I slung my jacket over my shoulder and joined the crowd. I was suddenly aware of the dust, the heat and the smell of thousands of bodies. There seemed to be an impossible number of people jammed into the small space. Once I'd entered the stream it would have been impossible to turn back. I was carried along, past the street vendors with their piles of sugar cane, fruit and vegetables and the stalls selling live chickens and goats and masses of silvery fish, slithering about on beds of melting ice, into the heart of the bazaar.

Once inside, the press of bodies eased a bit and it was possible to stop and take bearings. Remember, this was about thirty years ago and the mad tourist rush to every part of the world hadn't got fully underway. Nowadays, I imagine, there are lots of white faces to be seen inside the Pettah. Not so, then. I glimpsed a party of beefy, sweating men and women—Germans or Americans at a guess—being carefully shepherded by a guide in an immaculate white uniform, and a few other palefaces in ones and twos, gazing around them and fending off the shouting stall holders and lottery ticket-sellers.

The noise and dirt got worse the further in I went. Refuse from the operations being carried on—sugar cane peeling, bread-making, wood carving, spice grinding—was simply dumped into the streets. It was pushed into piles by sweepers but not collected, and the feet of thousands of people distributed it over the whole place. Betel-chewers spat red muck everywhere and it was impossible to avoid getting it on your shoes and pants. It was incredibly hot and my shirt was sticking to me when I located the Street of Gold. I looked at the map and discovered I was at the wrong end of it. I tramped on down its winding length, past the stalls and shops—just shallow niches in a mudbrick wall, selling gold statues, rings, chains and bracelets, gold-hilted knives, boxes inlaid with gold and books printed on gold leaf.

The sellers shouted, 'You buy! You buy!' I shook my head and kept moving. It was impossible not to notice how much darker most of the people were than the general run of citizenry in Colombo. Dark, and thin with it. The women were well swaddled up in long white dresses with wrappings over their heads and faces. They moved with an incredible elegance down the narrow, cobbled road, which was busy but much cleaner than the produce streets. The men, most of whom were bearded and none clean-shaven, wore long white shirts over ankle-length sarongs or loose trousers. Everywhere else in the town I'd seen the shaven-headed, orange-robed Buddhist priests, young and old, alone or in groups, begging, praying or meditating. There were none to be found here.

The Tamil children, of whom there were scores, were curious about me, trotting alongside for several steps, gazing up at me with their huge dark eyes. The adults ignored me as I kept moving and rejecting the stallholders' invitations. I had a sense, not of hostility, but of apartness and separation. I was the wrong colour, the wrong size, wrongly dressed. Everything about me was inappropriate as if I was the only person in civilian clothes on a military parade ground. It was an eerie feeling, like in some dreams where you are suddenly unable to stop yourself from behaving in bizarre ways although you desperately want to remain unnoticed. I also had the feeling that I was being watched while I was being ignored. Very strange.

I got to the end of the street, or at least to the point where it intersected with the Street of Silver. Not hard to determine. Down that way the intense light bounced off beaten silver bowls and trays and curved swords. The establishment on the corner was a proper shop, a separate mudbrick building, with a tin roof and window shutters propped open. It was given over half to gold and half to silver. A man standing outside looked at me without making the usual 'Come and buy' gestures. He was taller than the average Tamil, not much under six feet, but with the same build. He wore a shirt and sarong and his feet were bare. He was smoking a cigarette that looked extraordinarily white against his coal-black skin and beard.

I wiped my face and hands and shrugged into my jacket. I slipped up my loosened tie knot and approached the man. 'Good morning.'

A nod. Again, not hostile, but nothing like a welcome.

'I'm looking for a Mrs Tirrundrai. I was told I could find her here. Is that so?'

He didn't reply but flicked his cigarette stub away and reached behind him to draw aside a beaded curtain. The sun was beating down fiercely and I was glad to get out of it. I took off my hat, ducked my head, and entered the shop. The temperature and the light dropped abruptly and I had to remove my sunglasses to be able to see anything. The interior was gloomy and the goods for sale—inlaid chests, jewelled statues and ornamental weapons—only extended for a few feet inside. Beyond that were living quarters—a rug oh the earth floor, a low table, wicker chairs. I blundered forward, thinking I'd be glad of a sit-down.

Something white drifted in from the shadows on the left. I blinked, struggling to adjust to the light. The white shape swayed slightly in the way the slender Tamil women did and I caught a scent that nearly knocked me flat. I'd never smelled anything like it before—a mixture of oils and spices and flowers.

'Sit down, Mr Browning, please. I am Mrs Tirrundrai.'

I sat in one of the chairs and watched her glide into a part of the room that was illuminated by a chink in one of the window shutters. She was tall and slender, white-robed, with sandals on her feet and gold bracelets extending up both of her bare arms. She wore the Tamil head covering and all I could see of her face was a fraction of her forehead, arched brows, huge black eyes, a straight nose and her sculptured lips. It was all I ever saw of her features, but I remain convinced to this day that she was the most beautiful creature I've ever seen in my life.

She floated into a chair across the table from me and adjusted the white scarf around her head. My chin must have been down near my chest and I suppose I was panting. She smiled, showing snowy teeth. 'I have been expecting you, Mr Browning.'

'What? I mean, have you? How could that be? I only arrived yesterday . . .'

'And stayed with Mr Vasco Da Silva and ate curry last night and went to the British and Foreign Bank this morning. Now you are here. How can I help you, Mr Browning?'

That explained the sense of having been watched which, now I thought about it, I'd had several times since my arrival. I could have felt threatened, I could have got angry. I did nothing. Her extraordinary beauty and composure calmed me utterly. I wanted to smoke though. I got out my cigarettes and asked her if she objected. She waved her hand, the smell of flowers carried to me and the bracelets tinkled as she pointed to a small gold dish on the table. 'Please do.'

'Mr Pelham-Smith asked me to see you,' I said, expelling smoke well away from her. 'He said you could put me in touch with Ranu, his son.'

'Ah, yes. To what end?'

'He wants his son to join him in England. To be educated there, and so on.'

'I see. And did he tell you anything of the struggle here?'

'Well, no, not really. I'm not much of a one for politics. Just trying to help a decent chap out, you understand.'

'For a fee.'

'Look here, Mrs Tirrundrai, that's none of your business. I don't want to be rude, but I simply agreed to make representations to this young man on his father's behalf. Nothing more.'

Suddenly she clapped her hands and spoke rapidly in a language I didn't understand. Then she said. 'We will have some tea and discuss this further.'

I didn't want tea but I did want the opportunity to keep looking at her with the chance that I might see a little more of that wonderful face. Someone scampered away to do her bidding. I didn't blame them—I'd have done some scampering myself if she'd asked. I couldn't help wondering who Mr Tirrundrai was, lucky devil. I stubbed the cigarette out in the dish and leaned back in my chair. My eyes were thoroughly used to the light now and I looked hard at her, trying to guess her age. No luck. Like her muted voice, her half-concealed face was ageless. I felt a peculiar sense of calm in her presence and realised, almost with a shock, that my attraction to her had nothing to do with sex. Quite a change for the old Browning.

A flunkey came in with the tea things and went through the boring business of pouring and moving cups and saucers around. The stuff has always tasted like boiled bark to me, right from the first when my father, 'Wild Bill', used to brew it up in the bush and make me drink it. He laced his with rum, of course. Since then, I've been forced to drink it in drawing rooms, railway trains, on boats and in bedrooms. Give me coffee any day. But it was close in the dark room and any liquid would be welcome. I sipped and tried to look as if I was enjoying it while Mrs Tirrundrai gave me a lecture on the sufferings of the Tamils of Ceylon. I can't say I took much of it in. The long and the short of it was that they'd been there a long time, were a sizeable part of the population and were being given a raw deal by the top dogs. When was it ever any different?

My part in the 'discussion' was to listen and drink my tea, which I did politely, just for the sake of looking at her and hearing her voice—which was accented but not strongly. She made the words sound as if they should be pronounced that way and anyone who didn't was in error. I nodded and murmured affirmatively. She sat very still, using a minimal amount of movement to drink her tea. Her arms were exquisitely shaped and her hands seemed impossibly long and slender. After a while I found my nodding impossible to stop. I realised that I was falling asleep and that was the last thing I wanted to do. I tried to recall why I was there.

'Ranu . . .' I managed to say.

'Yes, Mr Browning *sahib?*'

I caught the full force of the sarcasm and scorn in the last word and wanted to protest. I was her friend; I'd do anything for her. All my bones seemed to turn to water and I slid from the chair towards the dirt floor, but I was asleep before I got there.

CHAPTER FOURTEEN

Bananas were perhaps my favourite fruit before I woke up in the back of a truck, bumping along a Ceylon hill road, with a couple of hundredweight of them stacked around and on top of me. Since then, they've fallen back in favouritism behind apples and grapes, preferably in the form of cider and wine. It was incredibly hot in the back of the truck and the smell was enough to make me wish I'd stayed unconscious. The flies liked the fruit though, and so did a dozen other different kinds of insects that were taking bites out of me just to vary the diet. I was tied hand and foot and something had been strapped around my mouth, keeping my teeth apart and permitting me to breathe, but only just. I sneezed and shifted the gag a fraction.

The truck jolted and bounced and the only thing I could determine about its progress was that it was winding about and going up. At every jolt, a rock-hard banana stalk hit me somewhere—in the ribs, the ear, the stomach. I wriggled and tried to avoid the bashing, but eventually decided it was better to lie still and try to ride with the motion of the truck. Brilliant strategy—my comfort increased by about five per cent. The flies buzzed noisily; the truck's engine was badly tuned and it whined and complained; the suspension and gearbox were shot. To say the din gave me a headache would be a lie. Pain knifed through my head and I closed my eyes, desperately trying to blank everything out—sounds, smells, pain, fear—everything.

Of course, that didn't work, particularly in regard to the fear. I cursed myself for getting involved with Pelham-Smith and the Tamils. I've always tried to steer clear of politics for obvious reasons—for every guy who wants something done, there's another guy who doesn't want it done, and vice versa. There are no safe courses. If you go with the strength you're liable to be snuck up on by the underdog, who just might get lucky. If you side with the have-nots, the haves are likely to pound you into the ground. In politics all winners are losers sooner or later, and some people can be losers the whole way through. Philosophy—in the back of a banana truck.

A banana leaf tickled my nose and I sneezed violently. This completely dislodged the gag, which I saw was my own necktie. I didn't know whether to laugh or cry. At least I'd be able to yell out if we stopped somewhere. Terrific. I'd either be helped or someone would kill me. A bit of blood wouldn't hurt the bananas.

I felt the air growing cooler and, quite abruptly, the shafts of light died from around the edges of the canopy that covered the truck. I deduced that I'd been travelling for seven or eight hours inland from Colombo. I hadn't mastered much of the geography of the island, but enough to suggest that I'd been taken north and possibly east, into Tamil territory. I was very frightened. Some people are terrified by black skins before the owners of those skins open their mouths. I wasn't in that category. Errol Flynn, after all, was a pure Anglo-Celt and you wouldn't ever find a more treacherous and dangerous bastard than him.

In a longish life (even at this point) of getting in and out of scrapes, I'd found the unknown to be the most disconcerting force. If you know what the score is, who you've hurt, who hates your guts and why, you know what to expect and can get ready for it. With a bit of luck you'll be able to minimise the damage or wriggle out altogether. But when you can't for the life of you fathom why someone's holding a knife at your throat or stepping on your neck, you're in big trouble. What had I ever done to these Tamils? Then the thought struck me that Mrs Tirrundrai could be working for the other side. And what would that be? The government? But surely they'd just have rushed me off to prison or booted me out of the country if they thought I was a nuisance.

No, it had to be the Tamils. But what could they want with me? Hadn't I come to deliver . . .? Then I remembered the scathing tone in Mrs Tirrundrai's voice. *Browning, sahib.* I was all adrift in a sea of confusion, doubts and fears. Now that it was dark the insects had ceased buzzing. The ants were still crawling around and taking the occasional nip, but I was getting used to that. I could wriggle and thrash sufficiently from time to time to avoid cramp but my hands and feet were starting to feel numb and I worried about the lack of blood circulation. What happened in that event? Gangrene? I started to panic and shouted several times to no avail. Eventually, the several glasses of cordial I'd drunk at breakfast in Da Silva's house and the doped tea got to me and I pissed in my pants.

The truck stopped and I was dragged out and propped up against the back wheel. Someone cut the ropes around my hands and ankles. They needn't have worried about me running away. I tried to take a step and fell in a heap. No one laughed, but no one kicked me in the ribs either. Insect-bitten, covered in banana-stalk sap, smelling of urine and with a throbbing head and parched throat, I was half marched, half carried through some inky jungle to a small village consisting of a cluster of huts made of woven palm leaf. A few kerosene lanterns hung from posts and I could see people busy at cooking fires and drawing water from a tank under a sheet of corrugated iron. I propped when I saw the tank and made gestures that I needed a drink.

It was only taking two or three men to control me. They were strong but I was so desperate for a drink I let them feel the full weight of me. One shouted something and a small boy came running with a half coconut shell filled with water. My arms were released and I was allowed to drink. People will tell you that a drink of water in these sorts of circumstances tastes better than French champagne, etc. All nonsense—it was just rainwater, tepid and tasting a bit of rust. It was welcome though and I was careful not to spill any. It dulled the ache in my head to a bearable throb and made me feel vaguely human again instead of like a thirteen-stone bunch of bananas.

'Thank you.'

The polite nod I got in return encouraged me. Who would pour water down a throat he was planning to slit? They hustled me into a hut where there was a pile of straw, a bucket and a fruit box. I was made to sit on the box and rope was produced.

'Oh, come on,' I said, 'don't tie me up again. Where am I going to go? D'you honestly think I'm going to run away into that bloody jungle at night? I give you my word I won't budge.'

My three escorts had a brief consultation. The one who had okayed my having a drink was now holding a lantern. He appeared to be the man in charge and I kept my eyes on him while they kicked it around. My watch was still on my wrist and I saw that it was almost nine o'clock. No wonder I felt like shit; travelling for ten hours or more in a banana truck isn't something I'd wish on my worst enemy, but right then I wished it on Aubrey Pelham-Smith. I was still wearing my suit jacket, although its tailor wouldn't have recognised it. I patted the pockets and found a crumpled, but almost full, packet of Players and my lighter. The talking stopped for a moment while I handed round the smokes.

Encouraging. The long black fingers of each man detached several. 'That's right, boys,' I said. 'One for now and a few for later.'

I lit us all up and smiled encouragingly, especially at the number one man. 'We are not boys,' he said.

'Sorry.' I puffed smoke. 'I was trying to be friendly.'

He dragged on his cigarette, sucked the smoke down and blew it out in a long stream. I was waiting for him to make a witty reply, but he merely cleared his throat and spat fulsomely through the opening that constituted the door of the hut. Not so encouraging. They resumed their talk and the only word I caught that made any sense to me was 'Ranu'. I heard that several times. I was bone-weary, light-headed and still thirsty. As well, now that my sense of smell was recovering from the banana assault, I was ravenous. The Da Silva breakfast of mango slices and hoppers was a distant memory. I had no craving for alcohol, which only goes to show that I'm not the booze-hound people have said I am. In my experience, and I've been forced into teetotalism more times than I can count, the absence of booze is bearable if it's absolute. It's trying to *restrict* your intake when there's plenty around that's hard.

Eventually they stopped jabbering and the rope was put away. *Round one to Browning sahib*, I thought. I was encouraged enough to ask the man who spoke English whether it might be possible for me to get a bite to eat and, following that, an explanation of why I had been abducted.

He sneered at me and spoke in a tone reminiscent of that of Mrs Tirrundrai. 'Perhaps you would care for roast beef and Yorkshire pudding, sir? With a jolly good claret to wash it down?'

He was a young fellow, not more than twenty, and indistinguishable from the others except for his command of English and the red bandanna around his head. The others wore no headgear. Like them, he had on a loose white shirt and floppy trousers and heavy leather sandals. He was as thin as a whip and his skin was several shades darker than club chocolate. His dark beard was closely trimmed.

'No,' I said. 'That won't be necessary. I'll eat what you eat.'

'I doubt that.'

'Try me.'

He translated for his mates, who seemed to find the exchange hilarious. One left the hut and the other two stood by the door and watched me as I tucked in my shirt, pulled the tie from where it had slipped down around my neck, and tried to tidy myself up. It's hard to do when you're in the condition I was in, especially with the damp, smelly trousers, but I did my best. Remarkably, my wallet was still in the breast pocket of my jacket. I took it out and began ostentatiously counting the thick bundle of rupees.

'Put it away, Mr Browning. No one is interested in your money.'

'Just a talking point,' I said. 'What *are* you interested in?'

Before he could reply the man who had left the hut returned with a plate of food and an aluminium beaker of water. The plate contained rice and several small piles of what could have been meat or vegetables. It was impossible to tell in that gloom. The plate was put in my hands and the beaker was set down on the earth floor by my feet.

'Eat, Mr Browning. You must be hungry after your long journey.'

'I am.'

As I say, I've eaten hot food in Mexico and the Caribbean,[24] and I know how to set about it. The trick is to eat some rice or bread or whatever else available that isn't spiced first, and begin with very small morsels. This sort of anaesthetises some of the taste buds and allows you to build up to more solid mouthfuls. You should resist drinking water for as long as you can, and then swill it straight down the back of the throat. A cooled throat is a cooled mouth— don't ask me why. I proceeded to put these techniques into practice. It was difficult because I was very hungry and I have an unhappy tendency to bolt my food (several of my wives have commented unfavourably upon it). But I had a good idea of what these lads had been up to and I wasn't wrong. The food was truly fiery and, if I hadn't gone about it the right way, I'd have been rolling on the floor in agony. As it was, I found it hard to chew slowly, swallow carefully, gulp down the water and show signs of enjoyment.

'Good, Mr Browning?'

My eyes were watering but I was damned if I was going to wipe them until I'd finished almost everything on the plate. There were no utensils, of course. With my fingers, I scooped up the last of the rice that I'd carefully preserved and chewed it slowly, rolling it around in my mouth, letting the saliva run and allowing the starch to coat the underside of my tongue. I finished with a long swallow of water that hit the back of my throat and worked its magic forward. I pushed the plate aside and let out a long, satisfied belch.

'Capital,' I said. 'Anything for dessert?'

CHAPTER FIFTEEN

They left me alone after that little display, taking the lantern with them. When I say alone, I mean that one man, armed with an ancient-looking Lee Enfield, sat outside the hut near a small fire with his eyes firmly fixed on the opening. Nothing wrong with an old .303—it'll blow a hole in you big enough to put a fist through. Most of the huts I'd quickly glimpsed had been constructed of panels of woven palm-leaf, but this one was of mudbrick. I kicked at a wall in a desultory way (I meant what I'd said about not bolting into the jungle at night), and it was extremely solid. I remembered that the thatched roof was several feet above my head and there was no way to get up to it, even if I'd wanted to. Fumbling in the dark, I used the bucket as I assumed it was intended to be used and lay down on the bed of straw. I was itchy from all the bites I'd suffered and would have been cold but for my jacket. At least there were no mosquitos. Someone once said that genius was partly a matter of sleep management. Maybe I qualify; I was asleep within seconds of my head hitting the straw.

One thing you can be sure of in a native village, and I don't care if it's in Mexico or Ceylon or Tanganyika— you'll be awake with everyone else at first light or earlier. The roosters start crowing, the kids start running about, the women yell at the kids, the men yell at the women. I'd slept soundly and, just for a few seconds, I lay comfortably, easing my way out of a dream wherein I was dancing with Vivien Leigh while Peter Finch was leading the orchestra and fuming. Then I remembered where I was and I jerked awake. A hard piece of straw jabbed me just below the eye. I yelled something and saw a movement outside the hut. My guard, who appeared not to have moved for the whole night, pointed his rifle at me.

I jumped up and blundered out of the hut. 'I want to see the man in charge here. I *demand* to know why I've been abducted.'

The guard stood and brought the rifle up to his shoulder. His black face was impassive; he closed one eye and his finger curled around the trigger.

'Okay, okay. What about some food?' I mimed the action of eating and backed off.

He waited until I was sitting on the box before he lowered the rifle and shouted something over his shoulder. I lit a cigarette and looked out at what I could see of the village—huts, dark-skinned, white-clad figures plodding, carrying bundles or flitting about in and out of the jungle shadows. Young and old, male and female. I was up in the hills somewhere. The early morning air was cooler than it had been in Colombo and there were a lot of birds screeching in the trees. If I'd been knowledgable about the birds of Ceylon I might have been able to place where I was. As things stood, I knew I was a nine-hour truck ride from the capital.

After a while, a woman brought some food and a sarong. She gestured for me to take off my clothes and drop them outside the hut. I wolfed down some fruit and one hopper and then climbed out of the stinking shirt and trousers, underwear and socks. I threw the lot, along with the wrinkled jacket, through the doorway after slipping into the cool and comfortable sarong. Then I finished the breakfast, passing on the tea and sipping the fruit cordial carefully before deciding that it was undoped. The food tray was collected and the dirty clothes were taken away. I came to the opening and poked my head out of the door but a different man toting the same .303 gestured threateningly and I withdrew.

It was hot and boring inside the hut. I smoked a couple of cigarettes, scratched at my bites and longed for shaving tackle, a comb and a toothbrush. After a couple of hours a woman arrived to take away the bucket. She returned after emptying it and handed me my clothes, cleaned and neatly folded. My belt and tie were missing and the jacket was still slightly damp. I indicated that I wanted to shave and wash, but if she understood she gave no sign of it. Her face was almost completely covered by a headcloth so it was difficult to communicate. I put my clothes back on and counted my cigarettes. Six left. Rationing time.

More waiting. Next, the young man who'd run the show the night before entered with the rifleman and one other. The third man was carrying a camera.

'Sit on the box, Mr Browning, please.'

'Why?'

'We wish to take your photograph.'

'Why?'

The .303 was jabbed into my spine and I sat on the box. The photographer busied himself with the camera's attachments and I lit a cigarette. This time I didn't offer them around.

'That's good. The cigarette is very good.'

'To hell with you.'

'Head up, please. Face the camera.'

'Fuck you.'

The photographer got off a couple of quick shots as I scowled at him. He left the hut and the other two backed away.

'Please,' I said. 'Please tell me what this is all about. I'm going nuts just sitting here not knowing what's going on.'

The young man indicated that the guy with the rifle should stand by the doorway. Then he squatted down a few feet away from me and stared into my eyes.

'You are English, American?'

'Australian originally. What . . .'

'I am Ranu Pelham-Smith.'

'Jesus. You're the man I wanted to see.'

'Yes, to persuade me to desert my comrades and our struggle and go to England. To attend the Oxford University and become . . . what do you imagine I might become, Mr Browning?'

'Well, I don't know. Anything, I suppose—doctor, lawyer, businessman. Oxford and all that—the sky's the limit.'

He shook his head. 'No, to be a white black man is not to be a man at all. "Look," people would say. "There goes Ranu Pelham-Smith, the smartest nigger in the Inner Temple. He's the chap for your coon cases. The first black silk at the bar." '

He was getting himself worked up, clenching his fists and grinding his teeth. Best to say nothing when someone's in a state like that, especially if he's got a trigger man with him. Very briefly, I considered belting Ranu a hard one and going for the rifle. The place didn't look like an armed camp. Chances were the .303 was the only weapon around. But I rejected the idea. Although I had the weight and possibly the experience on them, both were young and looked quick. I knew that these skinny little Tamils were strong. With Ranu getting into a lather, it was the wrong time for a move that might make my predicament worse. Calm was what was wanted. I offered the agitated young man a cigarette and he took it. Say what you like about the unhealthiness of tobacco, it's diffused many a sticky situation.

The guard looked longingly as I lit the cigarettes and I kept that look in mind. Ranu dragged deeply, blew out the smoke slowly and got himself under control. The funny thing is that, squatting as he was in a mud hut, long lank hair falling in his face, wearing a sarong and sandals, I could almost picture him as a pin-striped barrister addressing a court on behalf of a client. There was something impressive about him that couldn't be detracted from by clothes and surroundings. Another stray thought hit me—*he really would be an asset to the movie.* I waited until he'd smoked half his cigarette before speaking.

'Look, you might be right about all that. I wouldn't know. I don't vote, not interested in politics. I'm not a lawyer, I never went to university, Oxford or anywhere else. I'm just an actor. Will you please tell me why I've been brought here.'

He smiled, showing teeth the handsome Hollywood hunks would kill for. 'And been fed, had your clothes laundered and been treated decently. Is it not so?'

'As you say.'

'What do you think of the tactics of Mahatma Gandhi, Mr Browning?'

'What?'

'You heard me. Passive resistance, fasting, prayer, what do you think of these as means to achieving political ends? I see the question puzzles you. Very well. Have you heard of the Mau?'

'Of course. I was in Kenya a few years back. Very dangerous lot, the Mau. They . . .'

He interrupted me. 'Yes. They kill people. Which of these two forms of protest is the more likely to be successful, in your opinion?'

He was a born politician, circling round and round, never getting to the point. I shook my head. 'I don't have an opinion.'

He stood up. 'I am still trying to decide myself and there is much debate among us as to whether the Tamils should follow the passive or the violent path. I lean towards the former. That is one of the reasons for your mild treatment. But perhaps there is a middle course, which is where you come in, Mr Browning. You are being held hostage. Your release will cost the film company one hundred thousand pounds and this action will secure much publicity for the cause of a free and independent Tamil state in Ceylon.'

CHAPTER SIXTEEN

It was useless for me to protest that, while Fox or Columbia might have paid a couple of hundred grand to ransom Clark Gable or John Wayne, no one on earth would part with a single dollar to free Richard Kelly Browning. Somehow they had got it into their heads that I was an important man. It was something to do with the connection to Aubrey Pelham-Smith, as well as my association with *Elephant Walk*. The film had been widely publicised in Ceylon, leading the locals to think it was going to be the biggest thing since *Gone With the Wind*. I told them that I wasn't even acting in the bloody film, that I was just an advance production man. They didn't understand—or chose not to.

I ranted and raved and begged them to talk to Vasco Da Silva, who would set them straight.

'That man,' Ranu said scornfully. 'We would not believe a word from him. He tried to keep Tamils out of his cinemas. He is a bad man. He would certainly lie.'

I recalled Da Silva's unhappiness about my visiting the Tamil quarter. It was the wrong name to bring up.

This kind of exchange went on for a couple of days. They let me out of the hut to walk around the village (under guard, of course) and to wash in a stream that ran close by. I still had no idea of where I was, other than in the uplands. There were high hills all around the village. For all I knew, there might have been a tea plantation with hot water and a cocktail cabinet just over the hill. But that jungle was dark, dense and threatening. I saw several sizeable snakes down by the river. One day there was great consternation over a man who limped into the village with slashes on his back and legs. Ranu told me he had been mauled by a tiger. He might have been lying, but I wasn't disposed to put it to the test.

Every day dark clouds massed in the east, filled the sky and the rain fell. My hut leaked; my straw started to stink and I got very tired of eating curried fish, vegetables and rice and drinking fruit cordial. I gave my captors some of my money and they brought back a substantial supply of local cigarettes. Nasty, loosely packed things they were, but they helped to pass the time. My lighter ran out of fuel and I was forced to use what passed for matches—lousy wood, lousy phosphorus, damp striking surface. You can see how the irritation crept up on me. I asked for whisky, but Ranu wasn't coming at that.

I dredged into my limited knowledge of the bloody country. 'You're not Mohammedans, are you? What've you got against a drop of whisky? What are you, Ranu—a Hindu?'

It was the first question I'd put to him for which he didn't have a quick come-back. He hummed and hawed and I stored the reaction away along with a few other things. The fact is that he liked talking to me, exercising his English, trying out his odd collection of ideas on me and trying to make sense of the things I said to him. He was a nice young man, really, with good manners and a sense of humour. He was interested in tennis and films as well as politics, and I could talk to him on the first two subjects, if not the third. He'd been educated at an international school in Colombo and I've no doubt his father was right—he was university material for sure. I picked up a smattering of the Tamil language from him and the others, enough to understand some of what was being said in the village. Not very interesting in fact, mostly, 'Get off your lazy behind and do some work' and 'My grandfather said it used to be hotter at this time of year when he was a boy'—that kind of thing.

After about a week I lost track of the date but I discovered I'd been in captivity for twelve days when Ranu brought me two newspapers. One was printed in Singhalese and of course I couldn't understand a word of it, but I recognised the photograph. There was Dick, wild-eyed and needing a shave, staring balefully at the camera. There was no picture in the English language paper, just a short item under the heading: FILM MAN MISSING.

The disappearance of Richard Browne is concerning the Colombo police. Mr Browne was last seen entering the Pettah, where he stated he wished to 'look around'. Mr Vasco Da Silva, the film producer and cinema owner, said that Mr Browne had come to Ceylon to look at locations for the forthcoming motion picture Elephant Walk.

Mr Browne, 45, is described as being six feet one inch tall and of muscular build. He is clean-shaven, has a dark complexion and was last seen wearing a cream linen suit with a white Panama hat. Anyone with information as to his whereabouts should contact the Colombo police.

'It is a conspiracy of silence,' Ranu said. He slammed his fist down on the English paper. 'They have not even printed the photograph.'

'It's a pretty lousy picture,' I said, looking at the other paper. 'What's the story here?'

'Very much the same. A missing person report is what it amounts to—nothing at all about our demands.'

'I told you I wasn't important. No one is going to ransom me.'

Ranu said, 'I have to think,' and rushed out of the hut.

I had thinking to do myself. Was it a good idea to stress my lack of value to anyone? What isn't valuable is disposable, by definition. On the other hand, if I built up their expectations to gain time, the let-down when they were finally convinced that I wasn't worth a brass razoo was likely to be abrupt and damaging to yours truly. I smoked a few of the lousy cigarettes, drank some fruit juice and did some exercises. Not having had a drink for a couple of weeks and losing interest in the food had stripped weight off me. Walking around the village and swimming in the stream had made me fitter than I'd been in quite a while. Maybe I *could* grab the .303, make a break for it and cope with the snakes and tigers.

Nothing about the plan appealed to me, but I set myself to keep my eyes and ears open—to try to find out where I was and how far I might be from some kind of help. A couple of days passed. I cut my smoking to a minimum, continued with my physical activities, adding in a few sit-ups and push-ups, and trying to soak up every word of Tamil I could. I was getting sharp, no doubt about it, and the guys who were guarding me were getting slack and inattentive. I doled out the cigarettes, shambled around, looked depressed. The guards looked bored. They even said they were bored and I could follow enough of their bitching to get a sense of tension within the ranks.

Ranu was beginning to look harried. He brought me more newspapers and showed me that interest in my disappearance was trailing off. There was still no mention of the ransom. I could have given them a tip or two—told them that they needed a name, like the Tamil Tigers[25] or something such, and that they should send in a few signs that they were serious, like an ear or a little finger. But I refrained. There were two particularly good pieces of news in the papers. Billy Hughes had died at the age of ninety. I'd always blamed him for getting me into the First World War and I was only sorry the little rat had lived as long as he did.[26] Anyone who let himself be called the 'little Digger' without living through the shit and mud of the Somme deserved to roast in hell. Jimmy Carruthers had won the world bantamweight title from Vic Toweel in Jo'burg by KO'ing the champ in two minutes nineteen seconds of the first round. I cheered when I read that and the noise brought Ranu into the hut.

'What? What is that you are doing?'

I showed him the item. 'He's an Australian. Our first real world champ.'

Ranu shook his head and squatted on the floor. I put the paper aside and looked at him. I noticed that he'd lost weight, making him even more stick-thin than he'd been before, and that his expression was one of intense distress. I gave him a cigarette.

'We have to talk,' he said.

'I'm listening.'

'No, I mean, we have to discuss what is happening.'

'Ranu, I don't *know* what's happening. I'm a prisoner in a mud hut, remember? Under armed guard, night and day.'

'You have been a soldier. You've told me so yourself,' he said. 'And I've watched you. You are learning everything you can about this place. You are exercising and making yourself strong. You plan to escape.'

I didn't say anything. I hadn't got quite that far in my own thinking, or in the necessary plucking up of courage. But he was anxious to talk and I let him.

'The Tamil people have been very badly used in this island. Both the ones who came a long time ago and the more recent arrivals. Always the worst work, always the least land. Now they have outlawed our language. Those of our children who attend school will not be taught in the language of their parents. They will become foreigners to their mothers and fathers.'

That seemed to be putting it a bit strongly, but I could understand what he was saying. I'd seen a lot of it in America—Jews losing control of their kids, who refused to speak Yiddish or wear the *yamulka*. The same with Italians and Poles. They talk American, they are American—nothing to be done about it.

Ranu flicked his cigarette out the doorway, narrowly missing the guard. 'They do not trust me,' he said. 'Because I am not of pure Tamil blood.'

'Who's they?'

He looked at me and I could see the doubt, fear and vacillation in his eyes. Take it from an old deserter (as I was in the First World War), young Ranu was ready to give it away.

'There is an organisation,' he said. 'It is not very strong or well managed. There is much division of opinion as to tactics and strategy, as I have told you. I have argued against violence, but others are impatient. The ransom was my idea. We very much need the money.'

'No one will pay any money for me.'

'Perhaps if you wrote a letter?'

Crunch time for Dick. It was a way to buy time perhaps, but if the patience of Ranu's mates was running short there wouldn't be much time. My best chance was to work on the boy himself. I shook my head. 'I'm not valuable enough to anyone. The only person I'm valuable to is you.'

'Ah. So we come to it.'

'We do. The ransom plan is a flop. Everyone is disappointed. A bullet for me. You're the architect of the plan and you're not a real Tamil. Why not a bullet for you as well?'

'Yes.'

'*Or*, you can help me get out of this and in return I'll get you to your father in England.'

He sniffed and shifted his weight uneasily. 'Treachery, betrayal.'

'Ranu,' I said, and I put everything I had into the next few words, 'think how useful you could be to the Tamils if you had an English legal training. You don't have to live in Wimbledon and play golf, son. You could come back here and kick ass.'

'Excuse me, why would I want to kick an ass?'

'It's an expression. It means cause trouble, get even. You could go into parliament or something. Change these laws you're so much against.' I was speaking softly and I suddenly realised how conspiratorial all this might have sounded and looked. Ranu was leaning forward, listening closely. I shot a look at the guard, but he was busy excavating an ear with his little finger.

I coughed and folded the newspaper up to fan myself. 'Bloody hot in here. What about a walk?'

Ranu nodded and stood. He told the guard to follow us at a few paces. The guard hesitated and then fell in behind as we strolled around the village. It seemed to me that Ranu's authority was slipping, along with his confidence. There couldn't have been more than about fifty people in the village and most of them were children. Some of the men appeared to go away somewhere to work, others simply hung around. They had very little in the way of possessions, minimal clothing and I assumed that all the huts leaked like mine. A couple of the kids had nasty sores on their legs that looked ready to ulcerate.

'Look around you, Ranu,' I said. 'You'll never get anywhere with this raggedy-ass bunch. Use your brains, son. They're the best weapon you've got.'

'How can I trust you? You would give me up to the police.'

I shook my head. 'No chance of that. Not when your father will pay me four thousand pounds to deliver you to England.'

We were standing down near the stream at this stage. Ranu tossed a leaf into the water and watched it swirl around in an eddy before floating away. 'I see,' he said quietly. 'Yes, I believe I can trust you.'

CHAPTER SEVENTEEN

What followed happened so quickly that I'm not sure I caught it all. Ranu whirled, crouched and leaped at the guard. The next I knew the rifle was falling free and the guard was staggering back. Ranu picked up the .303, reversed it and cracked the guard on the temple with the brass butt plate. The man groaned and went down in a heap.

'Quick, help me to hide him! We have very little time.'

We rolled the unconscious guard behind a tree and Ranu threw me the rifle. 'I trust you,' he said.

I caught the gun and slung it, soldier-fashion, across my back. 'Okay, what next?'

He pointed upstream and set off at a fast pace. I followed, glad I was fit because the ground was soft and the incline was severe. After a few minutes we came to a rickety bridge. We crossed it and headed in what seemed to be a south-westerly direction. I had on city shoes, not the best footwear for the terrain, but I wasn't complaining. After being cooped up for so long it was delicious to be free and moving, even if I was in the company of what had to be the most impetuous youth in Ceylon. I fell a few times on the slippery, muddy track, but I kept moving and didn't disgrace myself. Ranu seemed to float ahead of me, almost jogging, stepping neatly over the roots and rocks that held me up or tripped me. I was sweating freely after a few minutes of this but my wind was good, and, for all the discomfort, it was good to have the rifle banging into my spine.

After almost an hour I was glad when Ranu called a halt. I doubt if I could have kept it up much longer. I knew better than to lie down, though. I rested against a tree and concentrated on getting my breath and not letting any muscles cramp up. I tried to recall when I'd last seen or heard the truck in the village. It was the day before.

'Where's the road?' I asked.

Ranu pointed. 'A few miles that way. We're going in roughly the same direction but at a safe distance from it. Don't worry, I know this district.'

'So do your mates, I assume, and I'm probably slowing you down.'

He smiled. 'Not so much. You are doing very well, Browning *sahib*.'

'Cut that out! What about the others?'

'They will be confused for a time. Then they will come after us. Some of them will wait for the truck. I hope you have still got all that money.'

The cheap leather wallet had started to develop mildew in the humidity and I'd taken to stowing the cash in my pockets. I had my driver's licence, Pelham-Smith's card and other odds and ends as well. The only things I was missing were my jacket and the Panama hat, knocked off by a low branch early in the escape run. 'I've got it,' I said. 'What's the plan?'

'There is a railway station not too far away. We can get a train to Colombo.'

'How long have you been thinking about this?'

'A few days. Did you notice the reluctance of the guard to do what I said? They were starting to lose confidence in me as time went on and the ransom idea did not seem to be working. Come, we must keep moving.'

I eased the rifle strap on my shoulder. 'Do I have to keep carrying this?'

'For a time. They may have sent a message ahead by bicycle.'

'Now you tell me. Okay, lead on, Macduff.'

'Shakespeare. I have studied . . .'

'Ranu, tell me about it later, eh? Let's get to that bloody train.'

We pushed on down the bush track at a cracking pace, only pausing to take shelter for an hour or so when the afternoon rain came down hard in the usual way. When the track gave way to a rough road and a tiny settlement clustered around the railway station came in sight, Ranu used his handkerchief to sponge the mud from my trousers. I took off my shoes and cleaned them up as best I could with handfuls of grass. Reluctantly I threw the Lee Enfield into some bushes. Ranu, nervous as a bad putter on the first green, giggled when he saw my expression. 'It only had one bullet in it, Mr Browning.'

'Jesus,' I said, 'if I'd known that, I would have dropped it in the creek when we started.'

'Yes.'

He was a deep one, Ranu. We kept our eyes peeled as we tramped along the road to the station. The traffic was mainly bicycles with a few motorbikes and donkey carts. I started when I heard the sound of a heavy engine, but it was a timber truck, revving up to take a hill. We stopped at a stall and, at Ranu's instruction, I bought a straw hat and a couple of string bags. We bought newspapers, some battered and musty books, sweets, cigarettes, some rice cakes and fruit and a few other things and stuffed them into the bags carried by Ranu.

'I am your servant, you see,' he said. 'So I must carry the bags.'

'Fine with me.' I eyed the station warily. It was a tiny, flimsy-looking affair, just a long mound of beaten earth raised beside the track and covered with a ramshackle tin roof. Very exposed, nowhere close to run to and hide. There were perhaps a dozen other would-be passengers, squatting in the shade with their bundles. 'How long to wait for the train?'

Ranu laughed, still nervously. 'This is Ceylon, Mr Browning. The train *should* be here in about twenty minutes, but it could be an hour.'

'Jesus! That's long enough for them to get here from the village.' Ranu shrugged. 'Perhaps.'

'I suppose that's your Hindu fatalism. Well, I'm not a Hindu and I'm bloody scared.'

'Keep your voice down,' he hissed. 'And keep your distance. I am your social inferior, Browning *sahib*. Try to remember that. Read a book, smoke a cigarette and try to look unconcerned and as if none of this is happening to you. Is that not the way of the colonial master?'

I lit one of the local cigarettes for which I was beginning to acquire a taste, and waved away some persistent flies with a newspaper. 'Don't ask me, son. I'm an Australian.'

Ranu sniffed as he edged away, but he couldn't leave it there. 'Australia has a colony in New Guinea. It is an island of black people you call fuzzy-wuzzy. Is it not so?'

I could vaguely recall Flynn talking about New Guinea, where he'd misspent some time before he got to misspend it in Hollywood. Not much of what he'd said had stuck. Conversations with Flynn consisted mainly of listening to his stories of women he'd fucked, fights he'd had and books he'd read. I was never much interested in fighting or books myself. But I seemed to remember that he'd spoken of police-boys and house-boys and 'Marys', so I guess Ranu had it all about right. I grunted in reply and turned my attention to the book Ranu handed me. *Tarzan of the Apes* it was, by Edgar Rice Burroughs. I was interested because I'd worked on *Tarzan Escapes* with Weissmuller and *Tarzan's Magic Fountain* with Lex Barker. Lex looked right, but brains-wise he'd have been better off playing Cheetah the monkey. I'd never bothered to look at the books but, there on that railway station, leaning against a rickety post in a patch of shade and being watched curiously by a bunch of black-as-your-hat Tamils, I became very caught up in the Greystoke story, so much so that I didn't hear the first blast of the train whistle and only took notice when Ranu brushed past me carrying the string bags.

It was a second-class carriage Ranu steered me to. The Tamils all moved further down the train. It was reasonably clean, with padded seats and leg room enough for an average-sized person but a bit cramped for yours truly. I was about to sit down next to Ranu when he jerked his head to indicate that I should keep my distance. I took another seat, lit a cigarette and pulled my hat down to shade out the slanting afternoon sun. Ranu had taken a seat near the back of the carriage by an open window. He craned his head to look out of it and I gathered, by the way he settled himself as we moved off, that nothing untoward had happened. It was a steam train, of course, very slow and noisy and some of the locomotive smoke inevitably blew inside. There were no other whites in the carriage, just Singhalese and Eurasians, who paid me no attention and gave Ranu a wide berth.

I kept my eye on Ranu, who was very tense at first but gradually relaxed and settled into his seat. He maintained what would now be called a very low profile, reading a paper, eating a banana and dropping the skin from the window and eventually looking as if he might catch forty winks. I took my cue from him. To judge from the people in the vicinity of the railway station and those waiting for the train, we were in Tamil territory where, presumably, Ranu's erstwhile colleagues had some clout. But here in the second-class carriage things were different. I was a free man with money in my pocket and a servant to boot. A whisky and soda would have been very welcome, but things had decidedly looked up. I went on with the book and I can't think of a story I've enjoyed more. I guess I must have been nervous without being aware of it, because reading isn't really my thing. Whatever the reason, it kept my interest. I ate some fruit and rice cakes when Ranu offered them to me, and drank some tea he got at a stop.

The train didn't stop often, but it was cautiously slow on the downgrades and it laboured hard on the upslopes and it looked as if the trip was going to take as long by train as it had by truck; maybe longer. We left the high country and I felt the air warm up as we got down closer to sea level. Just about everyone in the carriage dozed off and I suppose I did too from time to time, but not for long because I was keen to see how Lord Greystoke made out. I've often thought it, and reading that book confirmed the notion: all you need in this life is one really good idea. That Burroughs guy had made a fortune with the ape-man, just like Dr Watson with Sherlock Holmes.[27] I'm still waiting for my million-dollar idea, but I remember thinking that book-writing might be the trick and I resolved there and then to read all the Tarzan stories. (I have to admit that I never got around to doing that.)

Well, we got in to Colombo in the early hours of the morning and I was very glad to see the tallish buildings with their British look, even if they were all closed up tight. Ranu showed our tickets at the barrier and we joined the throng of people waiting for the arrival of our train and getting ready for the next departure. The trains seemed to run all night, so the taxi drivers were all clustered round and the food stalls were doing business even if the banks and insurance offices and other money-making enterprises were closed. I guess it was quieter than at peak hour, but it was still smelly, noisy and confused. After the tense quiet of imprisonment in the village I was glad of it. I sniffed the warm, moist air and wanted a drink.

Ranu shuffled up beside me and dropped the bags. 'I am in your hands now, Mr Browning. In Colombo you have the power, not me.'

I was jerked out of my feeling of safety and satisfaction. 'Do you think the police'll be on the look-out?'

'Not if what they print in the papers is true. As you said, you are not important.'

Clearly, that impression couldn't be allowed to persist. I fingered one of the wads of money. 'Not much chance of checking you into a top hotel, I suppose?'

He laughed. 'No chance.'

'Okay, then we're off to see Mr Da Silva, and he's going to give you a bed if I have to kick him out of his own cot, wife and all.'

'Da Silva, he is an enemy . . .'

'Ranu,' I said, 'you haven't exactly changed sides, but you're sitting on the bloody fence. That means you have to use anyone you can.'

We secured a taxi, although the Singhalese driver was unhappy about taking these two strangely matched passengers until he'd seen the size of my roll. Ranu sat silently as we drove through the quiet streets to Da Silva's suburb. It took me a few minutes of knocking to rouse the master of the house. He peeped out from the half-open door.

'Yes, who is it? What do you want?'

'It's Dick Browning, Vasco. With a friend. We want to come in.'

I heard Da Silva's gasp of astonishment. He flung the door open and came forward to embrace me. He was wearing a long cotton nightshirt and carried his usual smell of hair-oil, curry and cheap cigars. I stepped back. 'This is Ranu,' I said. 'He helped me to escape from the kidnappers.'

Da Silva's jaw dropped at the sight of the young Tamil, but he was equal to the occasion. 'He is most welcome then. Come in, come in. I am so glad to see you, Dick. You must tell me everything. I have been so worried.'

'Not worried enough to cough up a hundred thousand though?'

He ushered us into the sitting room and closed doors to seal off the rest of the house. 'Would you like some tea?'

'Bugger tea,' I said, 'I seem to recall leaving a couple of bottles of duty-free scotch here. That's what I want—a large one, and a decent cigarette, if you've got any.'

Da Silva bustled about, providing cushions and adjusting the chairs. 'Yes, yes. Whisky, of course. And what about your young friend?'

Ranu had arranged himself in a chair. 'I'll have a whisky too, thank you. Perhaps with a drop of water.'

It was my turn to be astonished. Ranu's accent was now purely *pukkah* British, without a trace of the Tamil sing-song. Da Silva produced a packet of Chesterfields from somewhere and put them on the table, along with ashtrays and a box of matches. Then he bustled away to get the drinks. Ranu and I lit up.

'So,' I said, 'you can be quite the Englishman when you want.'

'You'd be surprised. You *will* be surprised.'

I was still pondering that when Da Silva came back with a bottle of Bell's, glasses and a carafe of water. He prepared the drinks and lit a cigar. When everyone had taken in enough alcohol and tobacco to get us started, I said, 'What happened when I didn't come out of the Pettah?'

'I went to the police.'

'What did they do?'

'They went to the Street of Gold and asked questions. Of course they learned nothing.'

'Of course,' Ranu said. He'd finished his drink and leaned forward to make himself another.

'I received a note about the ransom. I also took that to the police,' Da Silva said. 'They told me to do nothing. I protested, but they said it was not possible for such a matter to receive publication and no assistance would be given to the paying of a ransom to . . . dissidents.'

'Did you advise London of this development?'

'I was expressly forbidden to do so.'

In a way, I was relieved. No harm done, as it were. Vasco and I could get on with our job and I could tackle the question of what to do about Ranu. He was starting on his third drink, I noticed. I was certainly planning to have at least three myself, but at a slower pace. 'When you advise the police that I'm safe and sound, Vasco, what will they do?'

'They will wish to interview you.'

'And if I say I was blindfolded the whole time and released without explanation, what will be their attitude?'

Da Silva puffed on his cigar, getting happier by the minute as I sketched out this scenario. 'I believe they will be entirely satisfied. Indeed, they will be gratified that their brilliant strategy has been wholly vindicated.'

'Good. That's pretty much the way it was, with a few small differences.'

'I am very happy that the matter should reach such a satisfactory conclusion. But what about . . .'

He gestured towards Ranu, inviting the boy to speak. But, whether through whisky, exhaustion or the release of tension, or a combination of all three, Ranu was in no condition to participate in the conversation. He had slid sideways in his chair and was fast asleep. Da Silva found a light cover and dropped it over Ranu, who stirred slightly and got himself into a more comfortable position.

'I never thought I would have a Tamil sleeping in my home,' Da Silva said.

I made my third drink, a light one, just to top me up. 'He's only half Tamil. I'm supposed to get him back to his father in England. It's going to be tricky.'

Da Silva peered closely at the sleeping figure. 'I see. Yes.'

'What do you see?'

'Nothing, Dick, nothing. Indeed, it will be difficult if he has no documents. But I am sure you can arrange it. You are a most resourceful man. Two of my daughters are in your room. If you will give me a moment I will relocate them.'

I let him do it—not gentlemanly of me, I admit, but I was too tired to care.

CHAPTER EIGHTEEN

If the kids ran around on the roof that night, I didn't know anything about it. I slept until late the following day. Ranu had awoken earlier, helped himself to some of my money, and made certain arrangements. Now he was offering me a cup of coffee, and when I saw him I understood what he'd meant about there being no problem protecting him from his former associates. The young man standing before me was clean-shaven with a short back and sides haircut. His skin was several shades lighter than it had been. His hair was dark brown rather than jet black, and in a shirt and tie and tailored trousers instead of the Tamil outfit, he looked like what he was—a smartly turned-out Eurasian.

I had to take a sip of the coffee before I could find words to say, 'Ranu, what've you done to yourself?'

'Not such a nigger as you thought, eh, Dick?'

'You cheeky bugger.'

He laughed and sat on the end of the bed. 'I got you some coffee. I know how much you hate tea.'

'Thanks.'

'For years I've stained my skin and dyed my hair. I wanted to be a real Tamil, you see.'

'I get it. And now . . . ?'

'Pretending is no good. Lies and deceptions cannot achieve anything. I wish to go to England and study law.'

'That'll please your father.'

His white teeth flashed. 'But he will be disappointed when I choose not to live in Wimbledon or St John's Wood.'

'I think he'll cope. But he gave me to understand it could be difficult to get you out of the country.'

'That is so.' A touch of the old Tamil defiance entered his voice. 'I am regarded as a dangerous dissident by the police.'

'We'll have to work on that. I imagine strings can be pulled. The big thing is to keep the police *and* your former comrades from knowing where you are.'

He shrugged. 'I doubt that anyone would know me, looking like this.'

I studied him closely as I drank the coffee. It truly was an amazing transformation, as if someone you always thought of as short had suddenly become tall. I would certainly have passed him in the street without recognising him, probably have sat down opposite him and not known. But that was just me. What was needed was an expert local eye. I got up, had a shower and a shave and called Da Silva in on the matter. He was looking a lot more relaxed in the company of this dark brown smoothie than he had with the jet black joker of the night before. We sat around a table and I ate a meal that was neither breakfast nor lunch nor dinner.

'What about it, Vasco? Would you recognise him as the man who came here last night? Sorry to do this to you, Ranu, but it's important. I have to get in touch with the cops soon. Do we put you in or out of sight? You see what I mean?'

Ranu lit a cigarette and leaned back in his chair. Again, I could see him at the bar or in front of the cameras. 'I understand. Mr Da Silva?'

Da Silva was not without his own sense of theatre, and made the most of the moment. He puffed on a cigar, surveyed the young man from this angle and that and eventually ate a piece of bread and an olive before making his pronouncement. 'I would say that, if he were to continue to shave closely, to stay out of the sun and also to put on some weight, he would be completely unrecognisable.'

There was some *dhal*, rice and vegetables and chutney left on my plate. I pushed it across the table towards Ranu. 'Eat,' I said.

Da Silva drove me to the central police station in Colombo and I made my report. I'm not sure whether they believed me or not; they would have loved to lay their hands on some Tamil protesters and they pressed me pretty hard on details. So, with a few variations, I stuck as close as I could to the truth. Of course, I didn't mention Mrs Tirrundrai, just said I'd been jumped on in the Pettah, knocked unconscious and taken away. I honestly had no idea about where I'd been held, and had paid very little attention on the train ride back to Colombo. The names of the few stations I'd seen hadn't meant a thing to me and I'd already forgotten them. As Da Silva had anticipated, the police seemed to be completely happy with the results of their 'do-nothing' strategy. I could understand that—it's a line I've often taken myself.

'Be careful, Mr Browne,' the officer who wrapped things up said. 'We would not like to lose you again. Perhaps you might consider hiring a guard. I'm afraid our meagre resources cannot run to such things.'

'Amen,' I said. 'And that's not such a bad idea, inspector. We just want to get on with preparations for the film.'

'That will be a wonderful thing. I wish you the very best of luck.'

I was chuckling as I walked down the steps from the police building. Da Silva mopped at his sweating face. 'I thought you handled that extremely well, Dick.'

'Listen, Vasco, there's no need to soft-soap me, okay? No one wanted any trouble. It's easy to handle things when they're that way.'

'I hope you will not be putting any adverse report on me in to London. I genuinely did my best when . . .'

'Don't worry. I'm all for a quiet life. Let's just get on with spending other people's money. It'll be a lot of fun. There's just one thing.'

'Yes?'

'Didn't I tell you to get rid of this bloody jeep and buy a proper car?'

'Yes, yes. I found an excellent French car. But when I came to take you to approve of it, you were not to be found.'

I laughed. 'Let's us go and have that drink we didn't get to have and you can tell me about it. But I'm glad you've still got the jeep. We'll hang on to it.'

'Why were you laughing before and laughing again?'

'Because I just thought of the perfect job for young Ranu.'

Ranu became my bodyguard and security officer. We tricked him out in khaki shirt and shorts with long socks and a Sam Browne belt with a Webley .45 in a leather holster. Under a sun helmet and at the wheel of the jeep, no one could possibly have recognised him as the wild-eyed Tamil of a few days ago. He wasn't much more than a boy, only nineteen in fact, and the whole thing appealed to him mightily. He was a terrible driver and needed a few lessons from yours truly to make him safe on the streets, but he picked it up quickly and we got him a licence under the name of Andrew Da Silva—a first step towards creating a new identity. We kept the food and drink up to him, but I can't say that he gained much weight—lucky young devil.

For those first few days in Colombo I went about very cautiously, keeping clear of quiet streets, staying with Da Silva and Ranu and keeping my eyes open. I got a licence for Ranu's Webley and for a Smith & Wesson .38 to keep in my pocket. We rented a house a few doors from Da Silva and I set up a sort of production office with a phone and a young Singhalese girl working part-time as a secretary. Ranu stood guard at various times during the day, and I stayed up a couple of nights with some scotch and the .38

for company just in case anyone took an unwelcome interest in the place. Nothing happened.

'Some people I know quite well walked past me today,' Ranu told me one morning. 'They were curious about my uniform and the jeep, but they did not know me. I am quite sure.'

'Good,' I said. 'I think we can relax on that score. I was thinking we should announce that we'll be hiring some Tamils to work on the film. D'you reckon that'd help to keep things quiet?'

'It would. We . . . they are not properly organised as yet. Any small gain is appreciated. Oh, I hate this. I want to . . .'

'Andrew,' I said, 'calm down. Take the long view. How long did it take Gandhi to get what he wanted? Twenty years?'

'Twenty years! I will be an old man.'

'Son, if you think that way you aren't cut out for politics. Forget about it for now, we've got work to do. How d'you feel about a trip to Kandy?'

'It is a nice town. I used to go there with my parents when I was young.'

'Good, you'll be a help. We've heard of a plantation that could be just right for the film. I don't suppose you know anything about elephants?'

'No.'

'Pity. I've got a feeling that elephants are going to be our biggest problem.'

He threw back his head and laughed loudly. It was one of the things I liked about him—his good sense of humour, which is to say that he often laughed at my jokes. I hadn't yet informed Aubrey Pelham-Smith about his son's new situation and attitude because I wasn't sure of how to do it. For all I knew, the mails and the telegraph could be subject to government inspection and in those days you had to book international telephone calls several hours ahead and at least half a dozen people in the system knew who you were calling. But I didn't know how long we were going to be out of Colombo and I wanted to get the message through somehow. Eventually I hit on the idea of calling Bobby Silkstein in LA.

'Dick, you old son of a gun. What can I do for you? Where you calling from? Hey, I'm not paying for this, am I?'

'No, Bobby. I'm calling from Ceylon and I'm working on a movie called *Elephant Walk*. It stars Vivien Leigh, Dana Andrews and Peter Finch.'

'Peter who? Never mind. What happened to the sea picture? Don't tell me, you got drunk and they dumped you. Well, listen kid, you're on your own . . . Hey, wait, you say you're workin'? I haven't seen a contract. Are you tryin' to stiff me?'

It took a while to calm him down and convince him that I'd keep strict accounts of what I was paid and that he'd get his commission. The names Leigh and Olivier were a big help. I asked him to phone Aubrey Pelham-Smith in London and tell him that his son was safe with me.

'What the hell does that mean?'

'Just do it, Bobby. Please.' I gave him the number. 'You can bill me the cost of the call.'

'I will, don't worry. Okay, I'll do it. Is he some kinda lord or what?'

'He's rich,' I said.

'Great. Hey, you hear the one about the flea crawled up between Betty Grable's legs?'

I'm proud to say that I hung up on him. We set off for Kandy, with me driving the beautifully sprung and engineered Citroën convertible Da Silva had discovered, and him travelling in the jeep with Ranu—it was necessary to put Vasco in his place from time to time.

Kandy was only about sixty miles from Colombo, west into the highlands, but it was a different world. The town was quiet and calm, with a river flowing nearby and the famous 'five hills' as a backdrop. No doubt about it, this was the place, and when we drove out to the plantation the impression was confirmed—rolling hill slopes, tea bushes, jungle in the distance. Perfect.

The plantation house was a gracious edifice with pillars, steps, vine-entangled pergolas. The Hollywood cameramen would wet themselves.

'This is terrific,' I said to Da Silva. 'What was all that crap about rough roads and rugged country? This is perfect.'

He shrugged. 'I did not know about the spending of money then. This place will cost, how do you say it? It will cost a bomb!'

'It's right,' I said. 'That's what's important. Andrew, unship that camera and get a few shots we can send back to England and LA. Where's the owner?'

'Who knows?' Da Silva said. 'I have dealt with the manager, who lives in a cottage on the estate. You will see that there are not many people working. The plantation has almost ceased production. The soil is no longer good. I have the keys to the house.'

'Good. Let's take a look. We need some wide hallways and a big space with a paved floor that can be made to look like marble.'

'Why is that?' Ranu asked.

'So the hero can play polo on a bicycle downstairs.'

Ranu stared at me.

'It's in the script,' I said.

CHAPTER NINETEEN

Things ran on pretty smoothly after we settled on that major location. Of course, the movie business being what it is, there were delays. Vivien got sick, holding things up for a while. A couple of people came out from England and found fault with the facilities for storing the film stock. Fans had to be installed. There was a spell of bad weather, holding up the recruiting of locals as extras and, of course, there were script changes and the squabbles that always go with a co-production. But we gradually sorted it out. I don't remember anything about Christmas, 1952—I spent it drunk in a very up-market Colombo whorehouse.

As the new year got under way the pace hotted up and I was kept busy supervising renovations to the plantation house, arranging vehicles and dealing with caterers and florists and all the hundred and one things that go on behind the scenes in movie-making. A wall had to be built and a set constructed for the elephants to knock down. Tamil agitators caused a bit of trouble, staging a demonstration here, breaking a few windows there, but there was nothing directed at us. I confess that I spied on Ranu, went through his belongings when he was away, kept track of the mileage he ran up on the jeep, but I found nothing suspicious. In the middle of January I received a letter from his father—something along the lines of:

Dear Browning

I have had a most extraordinary telephone call from a gentle-man in the United States who claimed to be acting on your behalf. As near as I can judge, the message he was attempting to convey was that my son was safe and in your care. I trust this is the case.

I am afraid that this individual made some scurrilous remarks about you and threw considerable doubt on your honesty. He seemed concerned that you would 'stiff'—American argot I understand for cheat—him of some fee to which he feels he is entitled.

I assume that you are observing security precautions in not contacting me directly, but I wish you had used a more civilised intermediary. If you have indeed succeeded in the enterprise, please send a telegram advising 'Deal completed satisfactorily' to the fol-lowing address . . .

I understand that Peter Finch is flying out to Ceylon soon. If, as I earnestly hope, I receive a cable from you, I will entrust him with a letter and other items for my son.

I sent the wire the next day and told Ranu that I had been in touch with his father. He took the news calmly and it occurred to me that Pelham-Smith might be in for a few surprises from his lad. Meantime, we were all on the payroll and life was good. Da Silva swanned around Colombo and Kandy in the Citroën, no doubt attending to *Elephant Walk* matters some of the time, but also look-ing after his other business interests. Ranu drove his jeep and played a lot of tennis. I played against him a few times and held my own through guile and a little cheating on the line calls, but there was no doubt that he had a considerable talent for the game. He looked good in his whites, and I could see him cutting a swathe through the girls at Oxford.

I developed some kind of intestinal disorder which took me into the hospital for tests. The few days' rest and bland diet seemed to help, and meeting Nurse Louise Townsend completed my recovery.

Louise was an Australian, working as a volunteer abroad—some kind of government-backed international aid deal. She was given board and lodging in a nurses' hostel and was paid a pittance. She was supposed to be teaching modern nursing stuff to the Ceylonese. She said she found them quick learners. The patients were another matter.

'Most of them prefer the traditional remedies,' she said. 'You know—herbs and poultices and such.'

'Could be right,' I said. 'A hell of a lot of people die in hospitals.'

She dug me in the ribs—easy to do because we were in bed in my bungalow. We had taken a fancy to each other in the hospital and when she found out I was an Australian, well, it just seemed like the most natural thing in the world for a couple of Aussies so far from home to spend a bit of time with each other. She was twenty-four, a big, blonde, healthy Sydney girl, who played a great game of tennis and was an enthusiastic bedmate. 'You know what I mean. There are some terrible health problems here, yaws and things like that, and spider webs and frog slime won't get rid of them.'

That was one drawback to Louise; she was a bit overfond of talking about her work, and nothing depresses me as much as illness, unless it's poverty. I could usually jolly her up with a beer or some tennis or a horseback ride or a good romp. She was going to marry a doctor when she got back to Australia so she was taking good care not to get pregnant. It was an ideal arrangement for both of us. One morning, after having stayed the night, Louise was on hand when the mail arrived. She brought it to me in bed, along with a cup of coffee. She was going to make that lucky medico a very good wife.

'I can't believe it,' she said. 'You've got a letter from Peter Finch!'

'So what?'

'So what, he says. I used to hear him on the wireless back home when I was a kid. And I've seen him on the stage and in a couple of films. He's . . .'

'Divine. I know. That's what every female between eight and eighty thinks. Well, stick around. Finchie and me are old mates and you'll be meeting him when he comes out to work on the picture.'

'Heaven,' she said. 'Does he play tennis?'

'I don't know. He rides bloody well and I'll tell you something else he's good at.'

'Oh, I'm sure of *that*!'

'Not what I meant.'

'What, then?'

I ripped open the letter. 'Drinking.'

'You're not bad at that yourself.'

'Not in Finch's class. What about a piece of toast?'

'You just don't want me to read your letter.'

'I'll give it to you to read if it's suitable for maidenly eyes.'

I've still got the letter. Neither of those snooty biographers bothered to get in touch with me,[28] so there are things about Peter's life at this time they don't know.

Dear Dick

I expect I'll be seeing you before long because the bullshit is slowly being shovelled away and we'll be off to Ceylon soon. But I thought I should put you in the picture a bit first (if you'll pardon the pun. I'm sure there will be a part for you, by the way).

The thing is, I've sort of declared myself to V and she's sort of indicated an interest. Trouble is, we were both pretty drunk at the time and I'm not sure she remembers much about it. She's been very sick but is on the mend and they say Ceylon will be good for her lungs. (She's got a touch of TB, apparently, which helps to account for her funny moods.)

But one way and another I wound up screwing that hellish bitch Drewe, and she's really putting the screws on me—threatening to tell V about 'us', although there isn't an 'us'. One quick root

*in the back of a car doesn't make an 'us', does it? I'll be counting
on you to get her under control when we're in Ceylon.*

*If all that wasn't tricky enough, Larry's threatening to come
out while we're doing the shoot. I've put everyone I can think of onto
trying to talk him out of it, but it seems the idea has taken root.
(There should be more words in this bloody language!) He suspects
there's something between me and V, although there isn't yet, and
he's jealous. Thinks he's Othello, probably. Maybe he won't come.*

*Aubrey Pelham-Smith has given me some stuff for you. Says
you've done a damn fine job. Glad to hear it, old chap, whatever
the hell it was.*

*I've got a feeling we're going to have an interesting time and
make a bloody good picture. Hope so. V has already said it will
be a great relief for her not to have to go mad, commit suicide or
contemplate murder. Of course, if Larry turns up we might have to
do all three. Hah, hah.*

*I've had the word that if this one's any good Hollywood will
sit up and pay attention. So I might be out there with you and
Errol in the bright lights and the big bucks.*

All the best

Peter

I showed the letter to Louise, who read it and tossed it aside
disdainfully. 'I don't think I like Mr Finch after all,' she said.

I said, 'He's an actor. It's a tough job. You have to make
allowances.'

'Tough? Are you serious?'

I shrugged. I'd never thought much about the demands of the
acting business, but right then, thinking about the victims like
Clara Bow, Lupe Velez, Buster Keaton, I had a flash of insight. 'It's
pretend, pretend, pretend. After a while reality becomes a problem.
Tell me something tougher than that.'

'You've got a point,' she said. 'We've got time for a couple of sets before my shift. What do you say?'

'Right. Pity you can't get a transfer up to Kandy.'

'Huh. From the sound of it, you're going to have your hands full with that hellish bitch, Drewe. What's so hellish about her?'

'Peter's being a bit hard there. Where's my racquet? I'll bet that little bugger Ranu has swiped it.'

'I thought his name was Andrew.'

'It's a long story.'

'He's very sweet. He's got a wonderful forehand, but I bet I could teach him a thing or two.'

She was a lot of fun, Louise.

The technical crew and support staff began to fly in and we moved operations to Kandy where we took over a hotel for the anticipated five weeks of the shoot. The technicians were all English because of a deal that existed then to do with the Technicolor process. All Technicolor productions shot in British Commonwealth countries had to use British technicians. This was to cause trouble later, but for now, people like John von Kotze, the colour expert, were pleased to be working on a big budget picture and wanted things to go right. The producer, Irving Asher, was an amiable type who wisely saw his job as keeping everybody happy.

The director was William, originally Wilhelm, Dieterle, a German who had moved from acting to directing and had got his start in Hollywood making German versions of American pictures. I can't say that I saw many of his movies or remember much about them, but he did a lot and didn't make a complete mess of them. He was no Billy Wilder, but he wasn't a Von Stroheim either, which is to say that he *was* a human being.[29] He was reckoned to be pretty good at the big, flamboyant sequence and that meant he was the man for the elephant charge.

They poured Dana Andrews off the plane at Colombo and I was there to meet him. Like me, he seemed to enjoy the heat and he brightened up, and sobered up, on the drive to Kandy. He pretended to remember me but I knew he didn't.

'Say, this is great,' he said, as we went through a bushy stretch with the coconut trees reaching into the clear sky. 'I don't get to do too many location pictures. I'm mostly sitting in bars with a drink and pack of cigarettes while some other guy's banging my broad.'

'Well, you're out in the open this time. You'll find Finch a good drinking buddy, though.'

'Yeah? I'm going to try to stay off the sauce if I can. I'm the clean-cut type in this one, right? Hey, isn't Vivien Leigh getting a little old for this stuff? Not that I'm objecting. She's got pulling power and I hear she's still a dish.'

I concentrated on steering the Citroën around the potholes and didn't reply. The fact was that despite Louise Townsend I was still carrying a sort of torch for Vivien and I didn't like what he said. But he was one of the stars, and you don't make enemies of stars if you want to keep on eating. If he said something like that to Finch he'd be in trouble. He was very pale, I noted, so the make-up people would have to work pretty hard on him if he was going to look right in Technicolor. Whereas, if they'd cast me, they'd have got a tan they might have even had to tone down. Ah, well . . .

Finch was the next big-wig to come in and I collected him as well. He looked tense but fit, and at thirty-seven, given his habits, he was wearing pretty well. A bit tired around the eyes, perhaps, but that's never been a detraction for a film actor. Cooper and Mitchum always looked half asleep and Peter O'Toole told me once that he actually *was* asleep during some of his scenes in his drinking days. Finch and I had a few drinks in the airport bar before setting off for Kandy. He gave me a heavy envelope and indicated a cardboard box among his traps that he said was for Pelham-Smith's son. I would gladly have told him about my adventures with the Tamils, but he wasn't interested. All he wanted to talk about was Vivien.

'I am *besotted* with the woman,' he said, over his second scotch and soda.

'Understandable.'

He shot me a quick look. 'You too?'

I nodded. 'From afar. Don't worry, I won't get in your way. But Peter, like you said, this is your big chance in the movies. Don't bugger it up. If you miss the bus in this game there's no guarantee another'll come along.'

'Don't I know it,' he groaned. 'Well, we'll see how it goes. I just hope to Christ Larry doesn't show up.'

'Is that still on the cards?'

'I hope not. He's got other fish to fry, but if Vivien gets sick or there's some kind of crisis, who knows?'

That wasn't good. From the little I knew of Vivien, crisis was her middle name. On the drive Peter began to relax and told me a little about his childhood in India. It was mostly about priests and ceremonies and mysticism, which was all mumbo-jumbo to me. He spoke well about it though in that magnificent voice of his and I knew he could have any susceptible female on her back with this sort of stuff inside an hour. He liked the look of Kandy, and took to Ranu who offered to drive him out to the plantation for a look around.

'I've got some stuff from your father for you,' I told him.

'When I get back. The horses arrived today, Mr Finch. Would you like to see them?'

'I'd like to bloody *ride* them,' Peter said. He was fresh from a long plane trip and a rough drive and he wanted to ride a horse. That was Peter—hell for leather. I left them to it and went off to steam open Ranu's letter and take a look inside his box. After all, I still had money to collect from Pelham-Smith and I wanted to know what was going on.

CHAPTER TWENTY

Pelham-Smith surprised me. I thought he might have sent the boy a long, haranguing letter about duty and family and all that rubbish. God knows what I thought might have been in the box—clean underwear? Instead, the letter was a calm, deeply affectionate try at winning Ranu's esteem and love. I almost felt ashamed of myself for prying as I read it. Almost. I'm a born snoop, so I won't pretend I didn't get some sort of a kick out of it. The father assured the son he respected his political ideas although he did not share them. He urged Ranu to study for a profession in order that he might be useful in the world. 'A driver', as he put it, not 'a passenger'. He wrote of his own study of the Hindu religion, undertaken out of regard for his wife, and his longing to discuss all these issues and more with his offspring.

Moving stuff. Then he got down to practicalities. He enclosed a British passport made out in the name of Ranjit Smith. I opened it. The photograph of the bearer resembled Ranu reasonably well—a bit rounder in the face and with the hair cropped even shorter, but not bad. Pelham-Smith said, without further explanation, that it was a photograph of Ranu's cousin and that in most respects the document was genuine. He also enclosed an airline ticket for Ranjit Smith from Colombo to London and two hundred and fifty pounds in cash. As far as I could see, there was nothing to prevent the boy from hopping on a plane any time he chose.

Then came the stuff that interested yours truly. Ranu was to inform me that I would receive the rest of my fee the minute he arrived in London. Fair enough. Then came some subtleties. The Oxford and Cambridge entrance examinations were held in May. Application forms were enclosed. Pelham-Smith wrote that he understood that Ranu might have matters to wind up and obligations to see through. He urged him to complete the forms and seriously consider being back in England in time to prepare for the exams. Handbooks from both universities were duly enclosed. The man was big on giving the boy a choice, although a limited one. I hoped Ranu hadn't set his heart on going to the LSE, which I'd heard spoken of as a hot-bed of radicalism.

The box contained the university handbooks along with a packet of family photographs that I didn't examine, and a selection of books—*A Passage to India, Cry, the Beloved Country,* and several volumes of something called *A Study of History* by one A. Toynbee. Pretty heavy-going it looked to me, but I assumed old Aubrey knew what he was up to. I put everything back together as I'd found it and deposited the envelope and the box in the room Ranu rated in the hotel because he was the security chief. He'd grown a moustache (that would have to go if he was to travel as Ranjit Smith), and he looked the part. I went away with a number of things to think about, but principally how to get Ranu on a plane. Four thousand quid was a hell of a lot of money, and the sooner I had it tucked away safely the better.

I wandered out onto a balcony to have a smoke and met Andrews who was doing the same thing. 'Feel like a drink, Dick?' he said.

That's how long those kinds of resolutions usually last. Andrews had been doing his share of drinking from day one. 'Matter of fact I don't,' I said. 'I was thinking of driving to the plantation. Finch is taking a horse ride out there. Maybe you'd like to come along?'

What I really wanted was a heart-to-heart with Ranu *after* he'd seen what was in his father's letter. But it wouldn't hurt to sound him out a little beforehand.

'Why, sure,' Andrews said. 'Kinda dull around here. I'll just get my hat.'

Andrews was a nice fellow and we chatted along happily on the drive. Andrews broke into song at one point—'The Road to Mandalay' I think it was—and I complimented him on his voice.

'Yeah, I can sing a bit, but I always kept it dark in Hollywood. You're likely to end up in those dumb musicals with straws sticking outa your ears.'

'I hear you were a bookkeeper, too.'

He laughed. 'I worked for Gulf Oil, but I keep that *very* dark. Comes in handy dealing with agents, though. Who's yours?'

I told him.

'Jeezus. I bet he's been stealing you blind. Lemme tell you how they do it.'

He smoked Chesterfields, took a few judicious swigs of gin and lime juice from a hipflask, and his talk was of Hollywood—the Brown Derby, the lots, Selznick and Goldwyn and Huston—and I realised how much I missed it all. I became keener than ever to deliver Ranu to his dad and collect the loot. I saw myself back in Hollywood with money in my pocket, perhaps with a respectable credit for *Elephant Walk,* and the friend of the up-and-coming Peter Finch. I felt like singing, too, but Andrews would probably have jumped out of the car in fright.

We found Ranu and Finch in the saddling yard. They had just finished their ride and Finch was full of praise for the boy's style. He and Andrews had spent a bit of time together but were still circling each other warily. Andrews seemed to know how to handle himself around horses, increasing Finch's respect. I left them sharing the hipflask and Chesterfields, and talking about horseflesh and the movie.

'Andrew, a word.'

'Yes, Mr Browning, sir.'

'Don't be a little prick. Remember who rescued you from the jaws of death.'

He laughed. 'Remember who rescued *you*! Peter is a very fine rider, and a good teacher. Why is Mr Andrews so pale?'

'He spends a lot of time indoors. We haven't talked much lately. Is everything okay with you?'

'Yes, of course. I'm looking forward to the making of the film. When does Miss Leigh arrive? Is she as beautiful as everyone says?'

'Is that what they say?'

'It's what Mr Finch says, and some of the others who have worked with her in Hollywood.'

Not recently, I thought, but I didn't say so. 'Yes, she's beautiful. Look, are you still planning to head for England when this is over?'

He plucked my Players from my shirt pocket, extracted one and lit it deftly. 'Don't worry, Dick. I know there is some kind of advantage to you when I reach England. I'll be going. I'm just not quite sure when. I am enjoying this so much.'

This wasn't too bad, but it could be better.

'Great,' I said. 'But don't kid yourself. People could still be looking for you and you never know who can sell you out.'

He'd taken to wearing a broad-brimmed hat to keep the sun off and his skin had paled to a colour not much darker than mine. The disguise was still good, but I didn't want him to think he could keep it up indefinitely. His hand shook a fraction as he took the cigarette from his mouth.

'What do you mean?'

'Come on. That woman I met in the Street of Gold, Mrs Tirrundrai. She wasn't any pushover. Your pals could be coming up with new plans all the time. What if they grabbed Da Silva? How long would it be before he blabbed everything?'

He was really edgy now. 'I did not think of that. I must watch over him. Where is he?'

'Easy. Easy. I'm just talking, just reminding you to stay on the alert. Well, I'd better be getting back to Kandy.'

He dropped the half-smoked cigarette on the ground and stood on it. 'I will come with you and see what is in my father's letter. I'll leave the jeep for Mr Finch and Mr Andrews.'

'Good idea,' I said.

Of course I was working on him and he was only a kid and I shouldn't have done it, but I had my own interests to safeguard. Here he was, only nineteen, and looking forward to life with a rich father and Oxford and Cambridge, sherry with the tutor, the bloody boat race, deb balls and all that. I had nearly three times as many years on the clock[30] and not many more grabs left at the brass ring. We drove back to Kandy and I told him I'd put the stuff in his room. He went off without a word and I adjourned to the bar for a contemplative smoke.

Vivien was due in the following day and the shoot was scheduled to start two days later. All preparations seemed to have been made satisfactorily. There were bicycles for Finch and his mates to ride through the (convincingly faked) marble passageways of the house; the extras, including some Tamils, had been engaged and Da Silva assured me that everything to do with the elephants was under control. That was one aspect of the business I refused to have anything to do with. We'd had a few nasty experiences with the brutes in Kenya on *King Solomon's Mines,* where a couple of the handlers had actually been killed. Experts can talk until they're blue in the face about the differences between African and Indian elephants—an elephant is an elephant, too big and too unpredictable.

I was mulling these things over when Ranu and Da Silva joined me in the bar. Ranu had had a terrible headache the day after he'd punished the scotch some weeks back and had sworn off liquor. He was drinking Coca-Cola, of which a big supply had been flown in for the Americans. Da Silva, sensibly, brought me across a scotch and soda and had a gin sling for himself. They looked like two worried men, almost as if they actually *were* uncle and nephew, worried about cousin Fred.

'Dick, my friend,' Da Silva said, 'we have a problem.'

I lifted the fresh drink in a silent toast. 'Problems are for solving.'

'I hope so,' Da Silva said gloomily. 'Ranu believes that one of the Tamils engaged for the film may have recognised him.'

'Jesus!' I took a gulp of the drink. I needed it. Admittedly, I'd wanted to put the wind up Ranu slightly, but I hadn't wanted him to start jumping at lamp posts. 'You didn't say anything about this to me before. What makes you think . . .'

Ranu's eyes were moist. I indicated to Da Silva that he should take himself off and he did, winking at me and patting Ranu's shoulder as he went. Da Silva always tended to overdo the body language.

I gave Ranu a cigarette. 'What's going on?'

'My father has written to me as you know. I am deeply affected by his words and the things he has sent. I do not want him to be disappointed.'

Me neither, I thought, but I didn't say anything, just nodded sympathetically.

'I am most anxious to go to England but I feel I should stay and fulfil my obligations here to everyone who has been so good to me. Mr Finch wants me to help him with . . .'

'Well, I'm not so sure about that,' I said. 'You've done a very good job as it is. I don't think anyone would blame you for going to England.' I almost let slip something about the entrance examinations, but I managed to hold it in.

He shook his head vigorously. 'No, a job should be seen through. But I am worried about being recognised and perhaps some reprisal being taken. If not against me, then against the film.'

There was no doubt about Ranu's capacity to think things through and see the angles. He was going to make a hell of a politician, if he lived long enough. It was a worry. I'd raised the spectre of the Tamils grabbing Da Silva and squeezing him for information. Now we had a possible double threat as far as I was concerned—to Ranu and the movie—under our noses.

Ranu swilled the ice around in the dregs of his Coke. 'I have much to think about.'

'Maybe you could get a message to some of the Tamils about your long-term plans. How you're still on the side of freedom and all that?'

'Possibly. It would be very difficult for them to understand. By the way, Dick, my father says he will pay you the remainder of your fee when I arrive in London.'

'Good,' I said. And that's where we left it, with Ranu fingering the Webley in its holster and calculating the odds. Finch and Andrews came bowling up to the hotel in the jeep, going too fast and sliding into a skid. I could hear them laughing as if they didn't have a care in the world. I was worried about Ranu and my money, missing Louise and anxious about Vivien's arrival. Monkeys chattered in the trees, sounding alternately angry and happy—not so different from the rest of us.

CHAPTER TWENTY-ONE

The location shoot of *Elephant Walk* was a struggle from start to finish. I knew we were in trouble when I met Vivien at the airport. She'd lost weight and was pale and fragile-looking. When she was at her best, she had a certain toughness along with the kitten quality. But there was none of that now. She was on some kind of medication for her various ailments and either this, or a couple of vodkas in flight, gave her a strange kind of brittleness. She kissed me on the mouth, a thing she'd never done before. Pretty solid sort of kiss, too.

'Why, Rich. How wonderful to see you. And isn't it grand here? It feels like coming home. I spent some time in India as a child, you know.'

I groaned inwardly. *Another one.* She and Finch could maybe go fire-walking together and talk to the monkeys. With her pale complexion and nervous disposition, it seemed to me that Ceylon would be one of the worst places in the world for her. It had got hotter and more humid and there were a hell of a lot of bugs and lizards and snakes about. There was also the press of bodies. Even at the airport, I noticed Vivien's alarm at the simple mass of humanity—the first thing you have to get used to in this part of the world. Some people never do.

We piled into the Citroën and set off for Kandy. Vivien got a wide-brimmed hat from a box and insisted that we drive with the top down. 'I want to breathe the air,' she said.

She breathed air for about ten minutes before falling asleep and I had a chance to examine her closely. I was shocked by what I saw. She was carefully made up, of course, but some of the powder and paint had come adrift in the humidity and I could see the network of lines beside her eyes and around her mouth. She was still what you'd call well-preserved, remarkably so, but the Technicolor cameras would be cruel to her. They would age her beyond the powers of the make-up artists to redeem. I thought about the script. It called for her husband to reject her sexual advances because he had all kinds of what we'd now call hang-ups. Could it work? She had a slim, shapely body. She would look oldish but sexy. I decided her looks could be a plus, if she could carry on after seeing the rushes.

We were stopped at a train crossing and she jerked awake. 'Why are you staring at me like that?'

'No reason, Miss Leigh. How are you feeling?'

'I'm fine,' she said in her Scarlett O'Hara accent, a trick she employed to make people laugh, usually when she was feeling lousy herself. 'And don't call me Miss Leigh. You don't work for me now. You're employed on the film, aren't you?'

'Production assistant. Maybe I'll get a small part.'

'Call me Vivien. We Britishers will have to stick together against these blasted Americans. You're really a sort of Britisher yourself, aren't you? Despite your LA ways?'

'I guess so. Australia's more English than American, though I suppose that'll change.'

'Yes,' she said. 'I remember Australia very well. I was out there with Larry not long after the war, you know. It was sort of a mixture of England and California. Tell me, Rich, how's Peter?'

She pronounced it 'Or-stralia', something that has always annoyed me, but before I could answer a riot broke out all around us. We were in a line of vehicles stopped at a level railway crossing, two or three back from the tracks. A train came through slowly, with the third-class carriages crammed to the limit as always, and people sitting on the roof. Someone fell or was pushed off the roof. People shouted for the train to stop but it didn't, not soon enough, and the person who fell went under the wheels. There were howls and cries and men leaped from the roof and began attacking people on the ground. Others jumped from the carriages and joined in. There was a tremendous amount of shouting and wailing and stones began to fly. A couple hit the Citroën. The thrusting, milling crowd seemed to be turning its attention to the vehicles.

Vivien screamed as fists drummed against the car. I slammed into reverse, revved up and tried to slew out of the tight space. I hit the car behind me but managed to get enough turn to spin the wheel and miss the one in front as I lurched out of the line. The manoeuvre enraged some of the rioters, who clustered closely around the car. I was terrified that they would start jumping inside so I put it in neutral, stood up and pulled out the .38. I bellowed, 'Get out of the way, you black bastards!' and fired three shots in the air. They fell back and I hammered down on the gearstick, swung the wheel and ploughed through a few of the stragglers until I reached the rough footpath that ran alongside the road. I barrelled along it, nearly running into a ditch, forcing people out of the way, with my fist thumping on the horn. When we got clear I was drenched with sweat and trembling from head to foot. I shot a glance sideways and saw that Vivien had gone into a dead faint.

A bad start and things got worse. Peter and Vivien fell on each other. A lot of pent-up passion being released, I suppose. It was hard to say who was the more obsessed and, since they were both highly strung and moody, the relationship was stormy. The booze didn't help. Along with Andrews and others they were both drinking heavily, never a wise move in the tropics. Finch and Andrews could handle it, but the combination of drugs, alcohol, strange food, the heat and the strain of filming, took a terrible toll of Vivien's strength.

Part of the trouble was that she and Finch were treating the shoot as a sort of working holiday. They went riding and driving and were late for calls. Some nights they camped out in the jungle and sat up around a fire, drinking and talking about Krishna and Shiva and all that jazz. Or so it was reported to me. I didn't go on any of these crazy jaunts but Ranu did, discreetly, and reported back to me. Grace Drewe presented another problem. Faced with the Finch–Leigh cataclysm, she was driven into a sulking, jealous antagonism and I believe she did everything she could to bring Vivien unstuck, in order to regain control over her.

Louise came to Kandy for a weekend after shooting had got under way and ventured the opinion that filmmaking was more boring that emptying bed-pans.

'And dirtier,' I said. 'Wait till you see two stars trying to hog a scene. What do you think of Grace?'

Louise shook her head. 'A nutcase. Watch out for her, Dick. One of these days she's going to do something dreadful.'

'She already has.' I told her about some of Grace's little tricks— losing make-up, spilling perfume, smuggling drinks to Vivien on the set.

'I mean *really* dreadful. And she's got her eye on Andrew. Watch out for that.'

You can see the fix I was in. I still had hopes of a bit in the film and I was dependent on Finch for that. But he was responsive to every whim of Vivien's and if she went on the way she was I could see the shoot being aborted. I'd talked to Ranu and he promised me to stay alert, to keep an eye on the Tamil he suspected and to run for cover if he had to. The last thing he needed was a distraction of the kind Grace Drewe presented. She'd thrived in the climate, had lost some weight and acquired a light tan. She wore thin blouses and tight shorts and lay around the hotel pool a lot in a fetching bathing suit. Dangerous.

As if that wasn't bad enough, *Elephant Walk* turned out to be what is called an unhappy shoot. There are lots of ways for this to happen—conflict among the director and the actors is the most common; actor misbehaviour isn't rare, and sometimes the director and the producer are at loggerheads. In the case of this picture it was simply that the personnel fell into two distinct and rather antagonistic camps. One was British, comprising the technicians, Finch, Vivien and a few more. The other was American, consisting of Asher and Dieterle, Dana Andrews and a few other Yanks in their entourages. It was nothing too serious—smart cracks, practical jokes, misunderstandings. But it didn't make for cooperation or smooth filming.

The weather was kind, in that it stayed hot and clear for most of every day and rained when it was needed. The Californians handled this all right, but it began to tell on the Britishers, who weren't used to such sustained high temperatures and humidity. Nerves frayed and unkind words were spoken. It isn't hard to see how I ended up in the middle of all this. I was a kind of half- breed, neither truly British nor American, and both sides aired their grievances to me and took out their frustration on me. After a short time it became clear that I wasn't going to get a part so I relaxed, considering that my work for the film was just about done. Let them worry about what to do with the elephant shit and how to get a piano tuner at short notice. I had my ace in the hole in the person of Ranu Pelham-Smith, now picking up a bit of money beating people at tennis and (to my relief) taking an interest in one of Da Silva's prettier daughters. She was staying in the hotel, supposed to be looking after her old man. Vasco was a busy guy, making as much of his involvement in the picture as he could, and he had so many daughters it hardly seemed likely that he could worry about the purity of all of them.

For a while I thought they were going to make it, but Vivien really started to run off the rails—crying jags, rages, insomnia, pill-popping and boozing to try to get steady and only succeeding in becoming more loopy. Not all the time—one day she'd be fine, the next impossible. A suite in the hotel had been rigged up as office and projection room for showing the rushes, but only a handful of people were admitted, not including me. I managed to get Irving Asher aside one day and ask him about Vivien's performance.

'You mean the way she acts or the way she looks?'

'Both.'

'She acts fine, sometimes. I'm afraid she looks old all the time.'

'She's forty, and Ruth Wiley's not supposed to be a girl.'

'She's not supposed to look like Finch's mother either. She looks great in the long shots, I'll give her that. I understand you've done some movies, why don't you come and take a look at Dieterle's work?'

What intrigued me about this conversation was that Asher didn't seem overly worried. You'd have thought he'd be tearing his hair out. I decided to take him up on his offer and look at a couple of scenes being shot. Louise was right, and the only thing more boring than acting in movies is watching them being made. I hovered around to watch a dialogue scene between Vivien and Finch against the background of the plantation.

Finch: You've no right to interfere.

Leigh: Right? I'm your wife, or I thought I was. Or something such.[31]

It went off all right, with no more than the usual number of takes, and the actors left the area. I was about to wander away when I noticed that the set-up wasn't being broken down quickly the way it usually was.

I saw von Kotze hanging around, looking unhappy, and I drew him aside. 'What's going on?'

'See for yourself.'

The cameras rolled and Francisco Day, the assistant director, supervised the reshooting of the scene *without* Vivien or Finch.

'Jesus Christ,' I said. 'They're taking out insurance. They can shoot it again against that backdrop.'

Von Kotze lit a cigarette. 'We're all sworn to secrecy about it. You can't blame them in a way. Some of the stuff has been unusable. It'd take a brilliant editor to pull it together. Do they have brilliant editors in Hollywood?'

'Some,' I said. 'If Vivien or Peter get to hear of this, all hell will break loose. How long has it been going on?'

Von Kotze was one of the Englishmen who hadn't handled the climate well. His skin looked yellow and he had a cold. He sniffed, sneezed. 'They're covered. They can use the long shots and put a different actress in for the close work. Just a matter of building sets exactly the way they appear on film. It hasn't been a happy shoot, has it?'

That was putting it mildly. It became quite common much later, double-shooting and playing around with the sequences. I heard they got two Musketeer and a couple of Superman movies out of the one shoot.[32] The possible consequences of what they were doing was frightening. Vivien would almost certainly quit if she found out and there was no knowing what Finch would do. The legal implications didn't bear thinking of. Time was running on and they were getting ready to do the elephant stampede sequence, the trickiest part of the shoot. A major blow-up now could jeopardise the whole thing.

I turned to leave and there was Asher, lighting a cigarette and blocking my way. 'Get the idea?'

I understood Asher's position but Vivien mattered to me more and I was angry. 'Yeah. Whose idea was it, yours or the Kraut's?'

'Look, we want her in the picture. She's a great actress and she's giving it balls. But we're worried she won't play the whole eighteen holes. You follow me? She's coming apart, for Chrissake!'

'She's tough. English actresses are tough. She'll get there.'

'Like I say, Dick. Can I call you Dick? Like I say, Dick. I hope you're right and we're doing everything we can to get her over the line. But you understand these limeys and we don't. Have you got any advice? Any tips? We're all in this together, buddy.'

I thought about it. Vivien and Peter were unlikely to be interested in the filming techniques; few actors are, and the security had been pretty good so far. There was only one major hazard I could think of. 'Do you know Grace Drewe?'

The reshoot had finished and Asher watched the breaking down of the arrangement of cameras, reflectors and shade boards. 'I know her. The blonde with the little jugs, hangs around the pool.'

'Keep her away from the set,' I said. 'And tell the people in the know not to talk to her. If she finds all this out you're dead.'

I was right about where the danger lay, but that was as far as my perceptiveness went. Things were quiet for the next few days because the weather turned sour on us, raining in the morning and again in the afternoon. This was ironical because the script called for a prolonged drought and there were dry shots needed that they just couldn't get. The locals said it had never happened in these parts before, but locals always say that. Ranu, who had his ear to the ground, said that some of the extras were muttering about luck. 'They are worried about the elephants.'

'Me, too,' I said. 'I'm just trying to tell myself they're better than tigers. How's Celestine?' This was Da Silva's daughter.

'She's a nice girl,' he said a little glumly and I thought I knew what that meant. 'She says she is afraid that Miss Leigh is going mad. Miss Leigh has been talking to her in a strange voice and addressing her in an odd manner.'

'Strange, how? What sort of manner?'

'Celestine says she sounds like a character in a play. She drinks a great amount of vodka and then she walks around saying, "I have always depended on the kindness of strangers." What does this mean?'

I shook my head. 'I don't know, but it doesn't sound good.'

I drove out to the plantation house and looked for Finch. I found him on a balcony with three cold beers lined up in front of him. He'd towelled off after doing one of his bicycle-riding scenes, but this was his real way of cooling down. I told him what Ranu had told me and waited for his reaction. He choked on the second beer. 'Christ almighty, that's Blanche's last line in *Streetcar Named Desire*.'

'She's on the edge, Peter.'

Just then I was aware of Grace Drewe standing near us. 'I heard all that,' she said. 'A lot you beasts care. D'you know what I've done? I've sent for Sir Laurence.'

CHAPTER TWENTY-TWO

It would be difficult to think of a potentially more damaging thing for her to have done. Vivien was on a knife edge between happiness and hysteria; Finch was in love, but nervous about blowing his big chance, and the whole film was skating along on very thin ice. Not an appropriate way of describing something going on in the tropics, but you can see what I mean. I should have met Olivier at the airport, and I spent the night in Colombo intending to do just that. But Louise was off duty and we went out and ate a lot of curry which meant that I drank a lot of beer and slept late. Louise was annoyed at my behaviour and attitude when I surfaced, some hours after Larry's plane would have landed.

'I could have come with you as your assistant,' she complained. 'I could have met him.'

I was giving the hangover the Browning treatment—white wine with soda water to wash down scrambled eggs, three aspirin to be dissolved in the drink. 'He's a prick,' I said. 'For all your outstanding assets, darling, I have to tell you that an Aussie nurse would matter less to him than a prickly hair in his right nostril.'

'Ugh, you're in a foul mood this morning. What an ugly thing to say.'

I went into my Bogart. 'I'm in an ugly business, sweetheart.'

'So what are you going to do?'

I shovelled in some eggs. She could cook, Louise, as well as do others things well. That lucky doctor somebody. 'Fuck him,' I said. 'Let him find his own way to Kandy.'

Well, he did, and he's written his own account of what went on in his autobiography, *Confessions of an Actor*. I took a look at the book in the Pasadena Public Library one time, and I guess old Larry put it down the way he saw it, more or less. Vivien met him at the airport and took him off for a drink, he says. According to Larry, he made the suggestion that she should be on hand for filming and this got Vivien in a rage. That was certainly credible from the look of the pair of them on arrival in Kandy. It was also clear that more than a few drinks had been had by both parties *en route*.

He's no fool, Olivier. He says that it was clear to him that Peter Finch was calling the shots as far as Vivien's conduct was concerned, and that he was torn between his passion for her and his wish for the film to succeed. Spot on, as we used to say in Australia. He picked up on the two lovers' Indian obsession and, like a wise man, knew he was on the wrong turf. The king of the West End was nobody at all in the Ceylon jungle. Give him his due, he didn't make a fuss, although his mere presence upset Vivien considerably. God knows what they talked about, Finch probably, and when Olivier says he couldn't work up any hostility towards Peter and that he'd always liked him, you can probably guess what he was writing between the lines.

I was holding my breath for the whole four days Olivier was around, waiting for Grace Drewe to pump some poison into him, for Peter to challenge him to a duel or for Vivien to go into a total collapse. They all kept very much to themselves for that time— holding up the filming somewhat—and it was hard to know what was going on. I managed to get hold of Grace one afternoon at the pool when she had finished a few laps of breaststroke for Ranu's benefit. He, I was glad to see, was deep in a volume of Toynbee and was also keeping well in the shade. Celestine appeared with the lime cordials and they got down to some serious giggling, so Grace was ready to talk, even to me, once I'd fetched her a gin sling and given her a Players.

I couldn't see any point in pussy-footing around with her. 'Didn't work, did it, Grace?'

'What?'

'Getting Larry over to screw things up. Mind you, I can understand how you feel; you're not doing very well—no part in the film, no screwing from Vivien, Peter or young Ranu there, very frustrating.'

She sipped her drink. 'You're disgusting.'

'You should ease up. You're trying too hard to be a manipulative bitch. I don't think it's really you, Gracie.'

'Shut up!'

'Only trying to help.'

'Help? The only person you've ever helped is yourself. I understand you, Richard Browning. I've seen the way you watch Andrew. You know who he is, don't you?'

To say I was alarmed would be a gross understatement. I was shocked; I could see my carefully worked-out plan being totally wrecked by this woman. I tried to keep my voice steady and my face unconcerned. 'I don't know what you mean. He's Da Silva's nephew, and very useful he's been . . .'

'That's nonsense and you know it. His name is Ranjit Pelham and he's a Tamil terrorist.'

Close enough, I thought. I managed a scornful laugh. 'Andy, a terrorist? Come on. He's just a boy. The sun's got you, Gracie. You've gone troppo.'

'Don't call me Gracie and don't try to laugh this off. Look.'

She reached into her handbag and took out a sheet of pulpy paper. It's lucky my heart is the strongest muscle in my body, because this was the second bad shock in a very few minutes. I was looking at a 'Wanted' poster. You know the sort of thing—a photograph of the offender and an account of his transgressions, a description, and instructions on what to do if you happen to spot him. I couldn't read the text, of course, but the name was clear enough—Ranjit Pelham. The big problem was that the photograph closely resembled the current Ranu—light colour, neat moustache, short hair. This time I had no chance of covering up my consternation. 'Where in hell did you get this?'

She giggled maliciously. 'Oh, it wasn't like that when I came by it. I got it in a post office and I worked on it a little.'

Looking more closely, I could see where changes had been made to the original poster. A full beard had been transformed into a moustache and the long hair cropped. Poor photographic reproduction in the first place had lightened the skin colour. I was never the world's greatest actor, but I'd seen a lot of the top performers at work and I knew enough about the craft to have a shot at pulling off a scene like this. 'It's amazing. It's him all right. How did you get onto this, Grace?'

I put a lot of sincerity and admiration into it, looking steadily into her cool, grey eyes. She wavered. 'Are you trying to say you didn't know? Why do you watch him so closely, then?'

'I've got my reasons. But you haven't told me how you sussed him out.'

She shrugged and drew on her cigarette and then let it almost burn away without puffing again. She was surprised at how close the burning end was to her fingers and she dropped the butt with a start. 'Damn it. I've burnt my fingers.'

'Cool them with some ice.' I plucked a cube from my glass and she took it gratefully.

'I went to art school for a while,' she said. 'One of our exercises was drawing members of the class and disguising their features with beards and glasses and such. I've got a good eye for that sort of thing and I recognised Andrew when I saw the poster, particularly the eyes.'

From gazing soulfully into them, I thought. My mind was at full gallop, trying to work out some way to cope with this threat. All I could think of was that Ranu had to be on the next plane out or he, and my four thousand, was in dire jeopardy. I finished my drink and gave Grace some more of the steady-eye treatment. 'I know we've had our differences, Grace,' I said, 'but this is very serious. We can't have a Tamil terrorist hanging about. He might decide to shoot Peter or kidnap Vivien. Who knows?'

She shivered visibly. 'Yes, I know. I didn't mean to blurt this out but you've made me so angry and I felt so, so . . .'

I knew what she felt—frustrated that she couldn't get her own way. Well, I know what's that's like and what the remedy is—somebody to promise a painless solution. 'Grace,' I said sternly, 'pack a bag. We're going to Colombo.'

'What?'

'Do as I say. There's no time to lose. We have to report this to the police. I've got some contacts there. They'll know what to do.'

'You mean, just go? Now?'

'The situation calls for action. If we leave now we can be in Colombo in a few hours. The police can communicate with their people here and arrest him. But we have to be quick about it and not let anyone here know what's going on. Come on, Grace, look lively! Grab what you need. I'll meet you at the garage in fifteen minutes. We'll take the Citroën.'

Of course it was a gamble, rushing her like that and mixing up urgency, alarm and resolution. But she bought it. She'd spent so long being stymied and defeated that she was anxious to be up and doing. I dashed off and found Ranu in the games room, playing table-tennis with Celestine. I yanked the bat from Ranu's hand and practically threw the girl out of the room.

'Grace is on to you,' I said. 'She wants to turn you in to the cops. I'm going to stall her, but you have to get to Colombo as soon as you can. Get rid of that moustache and catch the first plane to London.'

'No.'

'No? What the hell d'you mean, no? Do you want to go to gaol tomorrow? Goodbye father, goodbye Oxford, goodbye Prime Minister Pelham-Smith.'

He laughed. 'You are a strange man, Dick. Such big dreams for others, such small things for yourself.'

'Spare me the philosophy, sonny. You have to get going.'

'I am not going for at least forty-eight hours.'

'Why, for Christ's sake?'

'Because I want to see the elephant walk. I *must* see it, Dick. It will be wonderful, I am sure.'

What could I say? He'd been caught up in what was undeniably the most dramatic moment of the film (much more so than the conflicts between the planter and his wife and the rather tepid exchanges between the overseer and the Memsahib)—when the elephants, maddened by thirst, come down their age-old track, smash the wall and rampage through the Wiley mansion. I'd been looking forward to it myself, but not to the tune of four grand. I wanted to grab him by the scruff of the neck and shake him, but that would have done no good. At his age, romance was all and practicality was a bore.

'Okay. You want to see the elephant walk and you want to go to England?'

'Yes.'

'Here's what you have to do . . .'

Within the hour, I was driving on the Colombo road with Grace Drewe in the Citroën, talking flat-out, exuding confidence. I showed her the Smith & Wesson and told her how I'd used it to get Vivien and myself through the riot at the railway tracks.

'She didn't tell me anything about that.'

'She passed out as the first skull was cracked.'

Grace went pale and said nothing for a while. Then she launched into a diatribe against Larry, denouncing him as a heartless beast who didn't care if he was cuckolded and could never have loved Vivien to start with. A lot she knew. At my age, I knew that love could last ten minutes or twenty years, could collapse at a misplaced word or survive a hundred infidelities. It's the great human mystery, as someone must have said (I can't believe I came up with the phrase unassisted), and that is why it's at the centre of all the great stories. Tell me one that doesn't have it in there somewhere. I had other things to think about and didn't respond much after putting the .38 away. Grace was in a bad way, smoking the local gaspers one after another and muttering under her breath. I watched the odometer and slowed down as we rounded a bend where a track ran off into the jungle.

'Why are you stopping?'

'Sorry, Gracie. This is as far as you go.'

'Don't be absurd. What do you mean?'

Ranu emerged from the jungle at the side of the road pointing his pistol at Grace. He was resolute-looking, with a fair imitation of a scowl on his face, but nervous and a bit shaky. I hoped to hell he'd unloaded it the way I'd told him to.

'Andrew! How dare you!'

As I'd expected, her shock at seeing Ranu with a gun made her forget all about me, and I had time to shake some ether from a bottle I'd pinched from the infirmary onto a pad. Maybe she caught a whiff of it because she half turned, but not quickly enough. I got an arm around her chest, pinning her, and held the pad against her nose and mouth. She struggled, but she had to breathe and after she'd done that a few times she went limp.

'I hope you have not killed her, Dick.'

'No chance. She'll sleep for an hour or two, feel a bit sick for a while and then be ready to make trouble again. Let's get going.'

We left the main road and drove down some small tracks and out to the plantation where the elephant rampage was to be filmed. I'd noticed a couple of outhouses scattered around the plantation and it was my plan to hold Grace in one of these, keeping her quiet but fed and watered until the elephant sequence was over and Ranu could hop on a plane. I hadn't thought it out much beyond that. She'd kick up a stink for sure, but by then the whole operation would be packing up and who'd care? I was even prepared to buy her silence if the price wasn't too high.

Ranu was strung very tight on the drive and I chattered away, trying to relax him and, probably, myself. I was feeling the pressure, too.

'What did you think of Sir Laurence?'

Ranu sniffed. 'Impossible to say. The man was acting all the time. I felt sorry for him.'

'Don't. He'll make out all right.'

'Anyway, he left this morning.'

That was good news. We reached the plantation and I took the back tracks out to the building, little more than a shed, where the hellish bitch, Miss Drewe, was going to spend the next twenty-four hours, whether she liked it or not.

CHAPTER TWENTY-THREE

I'd been too cautious, and by the time we reached the shed Grace was coming out of the ether and I had to talk very seriously to her after handcuffing her to a work-bench.

'You're mad. You can't do this. Kidnapping is a hanging offence.'

'That's in America,' I said. 'It doesn't happen in the British Empire. Shut up, Grace, and listen.'

What I told her was the truth, or part of it. I didn't mention the size of my fee.

I could see her fighting off the ether nausea, getting herself back into fighting trim. 'Oh, that poor boy,' she said. 'I understand, Richard. Of course I won't do anything to stand in his way. I'm sorry I was so hasty.'

'I'm glad you grasped it.'

Ranu was standing outside, watching preparations for the shoot.

'There was really no need to go to these lengths.' She rattled the chain of the handcuffs against the solid leg of the bench. The bench was a plus for her. For all I'd known, the shed was empty or might have run to a few fertiliser bags for comfort. As it was, I could get her coat from the car and she could make herself moderately uncomfortable. 'Take these silly things off.'

'Grace,' I said, 'this is where you find out what movie making is all about. If they get through the shoot this afternoon, you'll be free by around six o'clock. But it's a bugger of a thing and they might decide to do it in the morning. You're here until it's done and Ranu's on his way to the airport. Got it?'

She screamed.

'Waste of breath,' I said. 'Especially with the elephants making all that racket.'

It was only fitting that the elephant charge, or elephant walk as it was called in the script, was the most dramatic part of the movie. The idea was that the elephants, about a dozen or so, but filmed to look like a lot more, should come down a rugged defile, mill around the wall and, after a bit of trumpeting, break through the barrier and stomp on down to enter the house. They were to knock down a chandelier—setting fire to the place, which they would well and truly trash in the process. The grand piano Andrews had played Mozart on was smashed to matchwood, along with 'the governor's' tomb. Vivien was to get trapped upstairs while the fire took hold. Finch, the hero of the cholera epidemic, along with Vivien, who'd cut bandages and sponged bodies until she was exhausted, swarmed up the ivy and rescued her from the inferno. Andrews was to arrive too late to be of any use, pretty much his role in the picture as a whole.

It was a bit like the burning of Atlanta, *Quo Vadis*, and *The Nun's Story*[33] all rolled into one. It was tricky stuff because the elephants had to be filmed *near* the plantation house but of course they weren't to smash it down, and the beaters and handlers had to be kept well out of sight. The wall was a set but had to look real and the sequence had to be shot right because there couldn't be any retakes, not with all that destruction. Some of it was absurd, of course. Finch had to keep a rifle slung over his shoulder. He'd used the rifle to wound a cholera-infected native who'd threatened to break through the quarantine. Great stuff, but it was nonsense to have him hang on to it. I suppose the idea was that he could shoot a few elephants if they got in the way.

Ranu and I took ourselves up to the 'bungalow'. I had it in mind to take up a position by a window, have a few drinks, and enjoy the action. I was about to enter the house when Ranu handed me the Sam Browne and his pistol and rolled up his shirt sleeves.

'What're you doing?'

'I've volunteered to be one of the beaters. It will be great fun.'

I was appalled. I couldn't see Pelham-Smith shelling out for a son delivered to him squashed flat. 'Forget it. You're crazy. It's too dangerous.'

He tossed his hat to me and I caught it. 'I'm not a child, Dick. Don't try to stop me. I want to do this to have something exciting to remember when I'm studying law in England.'

He turned and walked away to where the beaters were being marshalled. People were milling about. I spotted Andrews and Irving Asher going into the house through another door. There was no way physically to restrain him and all I could do was stand and watch while my four thousand pounds joined a crowd of poor devils who were working for a few rupees a day.

'Dick! Come on up.' Andrews was calling from a balcony and he had a bottle in his hand. I watched Ranu for a second, hoping he'd trip on a step and sprain his ankle. When that didn't happen I went upstairs to have a drink. Andrews was well ahead of me, which was no problem because he'd finished all his scenes. He was a real pro and I was told that they got the last scene, where he sees John and Ruth Wiley kissing after the bungalow has burned down and John is free of his dad at last, in one take. All Andrews had to do was say something like, 'Guess I'll catch the next boat,' and look resigned. He was good at that.

The bottle was champagne. I'd have preferred something stronger, but there were just the three of us and Andrews said he had another couple of bottles in a cooler.

'Should be a great show,' Andrews said. 'William's good at this stuff. Holy Christ, look at the size of that one!'

They were herding the elephants into position. One, the rogue bull that most upset John Wiley, looked like it could step over the wall. I have to admit that it was all done with great expertise and precision. There were a lot of cameras set up to shoot the sequence and, as I've said, the beaters and handlers had to get out of the way when their particular beasts were in shot. God knows how they choreographed it and there was no denying that it was dangerous work. Some of the cameramen would have to be quite close and as for the chaps like Ranu—it didn't bear thinking of. It's possible that the animals were partly tranquillised, but I'm not sure.

There were the usual delays and confusions and worries about the light, but eventually the signal was given and the elephants started moving and the cameras started rolling. Asher was quiet. He knew that it was the crucial moment in a shoot that hadn't gone well. Andrews chattered on about his next movie, something to do with tracking a man to Africa.[34] He was asking me about working in the dark continent and I was trying to answer while getting as much champagne inside me as possible and trying to keep an eye on Ranu. I quickly lost him in the swirl of huge bodies, collapsing masonry, falling trees and the dust thrown up by all this activity.

'Going well,' Asher said, and he took a small sip of champagne.

'Sure is.' Andrews set his empty glass down on the balcony ledge and reached into the cooler for another bottle.

It was an impressive site. The wall had been built to collapse, of course, and the set the elephants marched into would look much more real on film than it did now. The handlers ducked here and there, prodding and shouting and keeping the great beasts not only moving but showing signs of aggression. How they did that I don't know, but I have my suspicions. Ordinarily, this much action would have been shot in several sequences, but not this time. They had to get the lot—the elephant walk, the wall, the advance on the bungalow and Ruth and John Wiley's moments of truth—all in the one go. It was noisy and might have looked chaotic, but if you understood camera placement and realised how they could dub in music and sound you'd have got some idea of how well it was all going. So far, no one had been trampled to death and I thought I caught a glimpse of Ranu before a cloud of dust obscured him.

The flames started to flare inside the mock-up of the bungalow and I saw a stunt man (or maybe it was Finch himself, he was mad enough to do it) swarming up an ivy-covered pillar with that silly rifle over his shoulder. Asher allowed Andrews to top up his glass.

'Congratulations, Irving,' Andrews said. 'This is one of the great action shots of all time. Makes up for all the other shit we've been through. With a bit of luck you just might have a movie here, just might.'

'What do you mean?' Asher said. 'All we have to do is the set work back in LA.'

Andrews lit a cigarette, took a drink and looked just like one of the cynical, disenchanted characters he played. 'Doubt she'll get through it, buddy. Seriously doubt it. Lady's not a happy person.'

I leaned on the ledge and watched the set burn and the elephants walking about. The script called for them to walk slowly away with great calm and dignity and that's what they were doing.

All except one. Somehow, the big bull hadn't been rounded up and herded into line with the others. I saw him lumbering away and waited for the beaters to go after him, but none did. Asher and Andrews were chatting, addressing a question to me, but I didn't pay them any attention. The big elephant was bellowing and waving its trunk in the air. It was also heading straight for the outhouse where Grace Drewe was handcuffed.

It was a long drop from the balcony to the garden-bed below but I went over it without a thought, landing in the soft earth unhurt. Then I ran, shouting, screaming for someone to help me. I realised that I had Ranu's pistol in my hand. Great weapon against a twenty-ton elephant. I sprinted flat out down a path, jumped over flowers and rockeries, trying to gain on the elephant. The beast lumbered on, seeming to have only one thought in mind—to reduce the shed to kindling. Suddenly I was aware of someone passing me, moving more quickly, handling the ground better and not worried about the elephant.

'Ranu,' I shouted. 'Stop!'

If he heard me he took no notice. He was almost abreast of the elephant now, with fifty yards still to go. If he ran into the shed the likelihood was that the bull would trample them both. Then I realised that I didn't have the key to the handcuffs. I'd given it to Ranu. I ran faster, hard work in that heavy, hot, wet air, with the breath rasping in my nicotine-coated lungs. I wasn't really thinking, of course, but dreadful images rolled through my head as I ran—Ranu and Grace squashed flat, Pelham-Smith accusing me of murdering his son, a trial for manslaughter at best . . .

I caught up with the elephant and passed it. Ranu dashed into the shed. My momentum carried me on. I hadn't the faintest idea of what to do but I ran in front of the beast, shouting and waving. I must have pulled the trigger on the pistol. I must have pulled it several times. The shots that rang out frightened me almost as much as the huge creature coming towards me and made me scream like a banshee. I was almost outside the little building and the elephant was only a few yards away. Then time seemed to slow down and distances became distorted. The elephant trumpeted deafeningly, almost in my ear. I squeezed off another shot and its pace came back to slow motion, no comfort if you're expecting to be squashed. Then it lifted its head, roared, swerved and went past me, crashing through a brushwood fence and a bed of roses and tearing up a lawn as it headed for the jungle.

I staggered back a few paces and only the door of the shed prevented me falling in a heap. My knees were like jelly and my teeth were chattering so hard I had an aching jaw for days afterwards. The first thought that hit me, after I realised I'd survived, was that the .38 had been fully loaded when Ranu had pointed it at Grace. With a shaking hand, too. I managed to get my legs to support me and I opened the door of the shed. The two of them were twined together like something in one of those old Indian murals. The dirty ones. Her blouse was open and her bra was pushed up and Ranu had hold of one of her breasts. He was trembling almost as much as I had been. Grace's hand was inside his trousers and her tongue was inside his mouth. She was still handcuffed and the key was lying on the ground. I bent and picked it up.

I cleared my throat, not out of politeness but because my tongue felt like a lump of leather. 'I scared it off, so this's not the last chance you'll get. Undo the cuffs, son, and we'd better start thinking up a story, fast.'

They disentangled. Grace straightened herself and Ranu fumblingly undid the cuffs. They interlaced hands almost straight off and would probably have got down to it again if I hadn't stopped them. 'Any ideas, Grace?'

She was eating him up with her eyes. 'I . . . I was waiting here for Andrew and then suddenly I heard all this noise and he burst in and there were shots and then you . . .'

'Okay, okay,' I said. 'Got it, Ranu? That should do it. You look pretty bloody convincing to me.'

CHAPTER TWENTY-FOUR

I was the hero of the hour; an unusual experience for me and I must say I enjoyed it. Of course, I knew how to play the scene—very manly and quiet, looking surprised that anyone could make a fuss over something so perfectly natural. Thank Christ I hadn't ruined the effect by pissing in my pants as I've been known to do in moments of danger. It had all happened too quickly. It was one of those rare times when everything goes right. The business with the runaway elephant hadn't disturbed the filming. Everything had gone according to plan and everyone was happy. Asher took me aside to give me his personal congratulations.

'Dick, that there was the bravest thing I've ever seen.'

I managed a laugh. 'I reckon the couple of glasses of bubbly I had inside me helped, Irving. Didn't even think about it.'

'You've got guts, that's what it comes down to. But I want you to understand something. We can't let anything about this get out.'

That brought me down a touch. I'd already started to construct a fantasy around this incident. Whole careers in the movies have been built around slighter things. I could see myself getting the lead in an adventure picture or two—*Gordon of Khartoum*, starring Richard Browning, *Burke and Wills,* why not?[35] Asher explained that he'd have insurance problems and difficulties with the government if the story of the elephant getting loose and being shot at got around. One element in the story of the movie was true—the Ceylon government was very protective of its elephants.

'I didn't shoot at it,' I said. 'I fired over its bloody head, I think.'

'I know, but who'd believe it? There'll be a bonus for you, Dick, come pay day. You can be sure of that.'

So I agreed; everyone else was sworn to secrecy and the story of my amazing courage has never been told, until now. It's astonishing how the bad news spreads like wildfire and the few good things you do can remain a closely-guarded secret. Life is very unfair. But for the moment, it wasn't so bad. Andrews produced another cold bottle and we had a few belts before I remembered Grace's threat to blow the whistle on Ranu. I looked around for her but she was nowhere to be seen. I didn't trust her one inch, so I went looking. I managed to find little Ethel, Vivien's maid, who was packing up costumes in a room of the plantation house and asked her if she knew where Grace was.

She rolled her eyes and pointed down a corridor. Most of the house had never been used, of course, because the bulk of the interior shots were going to be done back in Hollywood where they could control the lighting and the sound and everything else much better. In fact I'd never looked thoroughly through the place, after establishing that it had the right exterior and ground level spaces for the shoot. I walked down the passage, not taking any particular trouble to be quiet, but I became more discreet when I saw a shaft of light slanting across from an open door and heard intimate murmuring up ahead. In fact, I was on tiptoe by this point. A gentleman would have retreated altogether, but I was never that, and with adrenalin still trickling through me along with other fuels like alcohol and curiosity, nothing could have kept me from sneaking up and listening.

'Oh, Andrew . . .'

'My name is Ranu, Grace.'

'What a beautiful name! And your body matches it. My God, I've never seen anything so beautiful.'

'Grace. Grace. Your skin, it is . . .'

'Yes, yes, kiss me there.'

'I thought I had killed you. I was sure the elephant would trample you and that it was my fault. I wanted to die with you.'

'Darling, darling, don't say that. Yes, oh, yes, that's wonderful.'

Well, maybe I would have snuck away at that point, but Grace suddenly went all practical. 'Andrew, Ranu. Stop! We have to be sensible.'

'What do you mean, Grace? Oh, please . . .'

'No. No.'

I was nineteen once, and I could guess at what those two words were doing to the poor young devil. I couldn't see anything, dared not risk a peep, but I could *almost* see, imagine anyway, how Grace was playing it.

'Grace, please . . .'

'I want you. I want you with all my heart and soul. But we can't let it happen, Ranu. There is no future for us. I'm nothing at all, and you are a fugitive . . .'

'Grace, Grace, my love. My father is a very rich man. I have a British passport. I have a first-class British Airways ticket to London. I am going to study law at Oxford University. My father will buy me a house. Oh, oh, they are so white, so lovely . . .'

'Ranu, yes. Oh, yes . . .'

That's when I backed quietly away from the door. It didn't look as if we were going to have any more trouble from Miss Grace Drewe. I'd parked a bottle on the stairs and I went back to fetch it before wandering through the big house, taking an occasional swig. I should have been feeling good. The four thousand was in the bag and I could look forward to a decent cheque from Asher in a few days' time when the shoot wound up. But the more rooms I looked into and the more I drank, the bluer I became. I suppose it was partly a natural let-down after the adrenalin rush, but I was also regretting my lost youth. I remembered when I thought nothing of driving 150 miles to take a girl to a party with the hope of spending the night with her. I remembered the excitement, the feeling of being prepared to do anything to get a woman into bed. Well, almost anything. I was never much of a one for taking risks with irate husbands. I remembered Nancy Barnes on the P&O liner and how we did it in a lifeboat.[36]

I was about to let out a long, satisfying belch when a hand clamped my mouth and nose shut and something very sharp pricked me above the right kidney. I nearly choked as the grip tightened and the sharp object went in a little deeper.

'Be silent or I will kill you. You understand?'

I nodded. It was about the only movement I could have made. The weakness was back in my knees and I was fast running out of air. There were three of them, all Tamils, all dressed in black, and they'd risen from the darkness without a sound. The one who'd spoken carried a pistol and he used it to indicate that I should walk down the passageway in the direction of the room where Ranu and Grace were plighting their troth. The blade left my back but I had no doubt that it could be put back.

The leader nodded and the hand left my face. I gulped in air and was about to speak when the pistolero shook his head. The third man, who hadn't so far done any threatening, took Ranu's .38 from the holster I'd been wearing slung across my shoulder with the Sam Browne rig attached. I was pretty sure it was empty but after all the confusion I couldn't be sure. The Tamil didn't seem to care. He fingered the gun lovingly and whispered something to the leader, who replied impatiently and in the negative. I'd picked up a bit of the language when I'd been kidnapped, but scarcely enough to follow a conversation. At a guess, this exchange was about whether to kill me now or later.

The boss-man carried the day and we began to move slowly and quietly along the carpeted passage. There was a turn to make and a short flight of stairs to mount before we'd be close to where I'd left Ranu and Grace. A couple of doors to pass which might or might not be locked—a slight chance to get in a punch or a kick on the stairs, but not against this toey little threesome, with their guns and knives and me quaking and still half-drunk.

They seemed to know where they were headed, indicating that they'd scouted the place not long before. I wondered why they hadn't just gone ahead and done what they planned to do. Then I realised that they must have thought I was a guard of some kind and had decided to take me out first. Good strategy. We were headed towards the back of the house, well away from where the elephants were being penned, where people were mopping up after the shoot and where Dana Andrews was probably still pouring champagne for anyone with a thirst. Back here, everything was quiet, and these crazy characters could do what they liked.

We reached the room and the leader peeked in while the guy with the knife reminded me of his presence. He dug in a little too deep and I couldn't suppress a yelp. That pushed things along. The two pistol-packers jumped through the doorway and I was shoved inside after them. Ranu sprang from the bed. He was naked and glistening with sweat. He stood, shielding Grace from the intruders. The leader barked out instructions I couldn't understand. The man standing behind me kicked the backs of my knees and forced me to kneel on the floor. I felt the knife at my throat and was sure this was the end of the line.

Ranu yelled something defiant and the leader raised his pistol. Grace screamed.

'I will address you in English, since you are not a true Tamil,' the leader said. 'You are to be executed for crimes against your people. On your knees, pig!'

Not good news for yours truly if kneeling was the execution position. Rather than kneel, Ranu seemed to grow in stature. He stood tall and spread his arms. 'I am ready to die, but you must not harm the woman.'

'A whore who has seen our faces? She will die with you, and this drunken one as well.'

I have to give Ranu full marks for guts. He shouted something that sounded very uncomplimentary and launched himself straight at the man with the gun. I closed my eyes and heard a shot, expecting not to hear the next one. Instead of oblivion, there was a scuffling and more shots, shouts, screams from Grace. I heard a grunt and the breath rush from the body of the man nearest me, so I threw myself sideways and rolled, still not looking. There was another shot and I was still alive and unwounded. I opened my eyes to the stink of cordite in the air and to see the three Tamils sprawled in attitudes that meant they weren't ever going to move again.

Two Singhalese were bending over the bodies. Grace, naked and rosy, was being clutched by Ranu. The knife that had been held at my throat was lying on the floor. I scrambled to my feet as Vasco Da Silva entered the room. He nodded approvingly and told Ranu to get his clothes on and take himself and his lady friend off to the airport at once. Ranu gaped.

'Do it!' Da Silva barked.

Ranu and Grace dressed hurriedly and departed. Neither gave me more than a glance. It was as if they thought I'd brought in the Tamils. Somehow I managed to get a cigarette lit and to speak in an almost normal tone of voice. 'Vasco, what the hell is going on? Who are these guys?'

'Dick, my friend,' Da Silva said, 'things aren't always what they seem. I've got some pals in the security service here. We struck a deal—trade Ranu for a couple of the Tamil hot-heads.' He pointed his unlit cigar at the leader of the group. 'Him, for example. They wanted him badly.'

'Ranu thought he'd been spotted.'

'He was, by the one who had hold of you, but it took a while for them to come after him. These excellent chaps were keeping an eye on things. They were very worried when that bloody elephant looked like messing everything up.'

'A deal, you said. You mean Ranu walks away?'

'Absolutely. Just between you and me, they're happy to see him go. Excuse me, I have to help them clean up here.'

I was still having trouble absorbing the information. 'Were you in this all along?'

Da Silva laughed. 'Don't ask, Dick. But I'll tell you one thing, I'm happy to put a few thousand miles between that Tamil bastard and my daughter. Why don't you go and find yourself a drink?'

CHAPTER TWENTY-FIVE

I staggered away, relocated my bottle and was trying to get drunk again when I found myself outside the house, standing in front of the set that had been used for the blazing bungalow sequence. Of course, it's mostly faked that sort of thing—done with gas jets from concealed canisters, smoke machines using cooking oil and trick lighting. But in this case there had been a certain amount of real combustion, and there was a smoky haze and a smell of burnt paint in the air. I lit a cigarette and looked at the set, thinking what a waste of time and talent all this was, when I heard my name being called.

'Dick, Dick, old man. What the hell are you doing?'

'His name's Rich, Peter. He's my Rich. The best motorcar driver and elephant handler east of Suez.'

It was Finch and Vivien, arm in arm, coming towards me across the lawn. They were both holding glasses and neither was anything like sober. The weird thing was, they were both wearing semi-Indian costume—Vivien in a silver and gold sari with a daub of paint on her forehead and Finch in a long white shirt over an ankle-length sarong. He had something wrapped around his head like a badly constructed turban. I took a last drink from my champagne bottle and threw it at the smouldering set. It hit something hard, and broke. I sat down on the grass, which had become wet from the water used to put out the fire.

'Life is a puzzle,' I said. 'A total puzzle.'

'No,' Vivien said, very serious. 'No, life is wonderful. Isn't it, Peter?'

'Wonderful,' Finch said.

I wasn't in the mood for any more of this. 'Where's Sir Larry?'

Finch laughed. 'He's gone. That's why life is wonderful.'

Vivien wasn't as drunk as Peter, but she was operating on a different plane, which amounted to pretty much the same thing. 'He hasn't gone,' she said. 'He's just not here.'

'Right,' Finch said. 'Dick, we're going to a fire-walking ceremony. You have to come with us. It's amazing. I insist that you come.'

'Now?' I said.

Finch took the cigarette from me, drew on it and threw it away. 'Of course, now. It's night, isn't it? Can't be spiritual in the daytime.'

'Spiritual?'

'You're at a very low ebb, old son. Personal energy's way down. I can feel it. Can't you, my dear?'.

Vivien nodded, somehow managing to keep the drapery over her head in place. Finch hauled me to my feet and we all staggered off towards the front of the house where a horse-drawn cart was standing.

'Can't go in a motor car,' Finch said.

I grinned. 'Not spiritual?'

'That's right.' He managed to hand Vivien up onto a seat in the cart and to climb aboard himself. I doubted whether I could make it but somehow I did. We set off down the drive and I have to admit that there was something soothing about the clip-clop of the horse's hooves and the flicking sound of the driver's whip as he urged them along. The rushing air was cooling on the skin and I began to feel better—not sober by a long way, but sensible enough to take an interest in what was happening.

'Where are we going, Peter?'

'To a temple on a hill near here,' Finch intoned with the million dollar voice working well despite the grog he had on board. 'Very sacred place. Just heard about it today. Seemed to be the right thing to do after . . . everything. Not for tourists, you understand. Only for the enlightened.'

'Are you enlightened?'

Vivien's slightly wrinkled, heavily be-ringed hand crept up Finch's arm like a glittering snake. 'We're trying to be, Rich. We're trying.'

I think they believed what they were saying, even though lust and alcohol and, in Vivien's case, other drugs were playing a bigger part in their emotions than spirituality. I'm not a very spiritual person myself, as you will have gathered. In fact a very little spirituality goes a long way with me, as Michael Caine says in *Alfie*.[37] (God, I would have loved to have played that part.)

We drove on through the soft, velvety night. Finch and Vivien were murmuring to each other and I might have dozed off a few times. When we stopped we were in a clearing with thick jungle all around. A small Buddhist temple was outlined against the night sky and there were quite a few yellow-robed figures among the people grouped around the fire-pit. Music was playing and the air was full of the smell of incense. Some of the people were swaying in a kind of dance and others kept up a rhythmic chanting that seemed to block out all thought and analysis.

'Isn't this wonderful?' Vivien said, clutching at Finch's arm.

I wasn't so sure. I felt a mixture of fear and resignation, as if everything that was going to happen was inevitable and nothing could be done to change it even if I had wanted to. We were instructed to remove our shoes and socks, leaving me in my *pukka sahib* shorts, and led to a position near the fire-pit and invited to toss bits of dry grass onto the coals. Peter threw a handful and it disappeared in a puff of smoke. The odd thing was that the bed of glowing coals didn't seem to be giving off much heat, but the flaring grass was convincing enough.

'Bloody hot,' I muttered, squatting down.

'Ssh, Rich,' Vivien whispered. 'This is a religious ceremony. It's like being in church.'

Being in church usually put me to sleep and, indeed, with all the incense and music and chanting, I was close to nodding off again. Someone threw some water on the coals and a cloud of hissing steam rose into the air. That brought me wide awake.

'Here they come,' Finch said.

A procession wound its way through the crowd down towards the pit. There were eight men, ranging in age from youths to bent-backed ancients. They wore sarongs that came to just below their knees and were bare-chested apart from garlands of flowers that hung around their necks. Their faces were daubed and streaked with white paint. They wore flowers in their hair, with the exception of one old boy who was bald. They carried carved sticks, which they tapped against the open palm of the free hand. More water and handfuls of something else were thrown on the fire and the smell of incense and herbs became almost overpowering. My eyes began to water and I watched the proceedings through a stinging, salty film.

The chanting increased in volume and tempo, the drum beat kept time, the bed of coals crackled as insects and bits of floating grass were consumed. The men walked around the pit, which was about two-thirds the length and twice the width of a cricket pitch. I stared at their faces as they passed close to me the first time. Their eyes were wide and fixed on some point in the far distance; their lips were moving in a low, humming chant and sweat was pouring from their foreheads. They completed one circuit and began another. This time I looked at their feet—bare, of course, with no sign of any protective ointment or covering.

It was hard to look away but I managed to shoot a glance at Vivien and Finch. Both were fascinated, utterly still, mouths open. Then the first man stepped onto the coals and I heard myself draw a breath. I was aware of the sweat running down my face and that I was swaying slightly to the rhythm of the chant and the tapping sticks.

The firewalkers, young and old, did not hesitate—they stepped from the grass onto the coals and walked slowly down the middle of the pit. At the end the group split into two—four turned right, four turned left and they returned along the edge. More incense and herbs were thrown as the men stepped out of the pit.

I realised that I'd been swaying and holding my breath. Now I took in a deep lungful and felt the heated, scented air rush through me. My face and shirt were saturated. The shirt that had been stuck to my back by dried blood now hung free. There was a roaring in my ears as if the chanting was going on inside my skull. To my amazement I found myself standing up and, along with a few other people, moving towards the end of the pit. I didn't think about what I was about to do and I was untroubled by it. It was as if I was outside my body, indifferent to what happened to it, and resolved to have this experience. I was aware of almost nothing except a magnetic force drawing me to the coals. Like the others, I was handed a carved stick and I began to tap it as we filed towards the pit.

I wasn't the first in line and I wasn't the last. We did the two turns around the coals the way the others had done, drawing a little nearer each time. Flowers were dropped over our heads. The man in front of me ambled onto the dark, rough, unevenly glowing surface and I followed him like a soldier marching in step. A delicious feeling rose inside me, something like the effect of good marijuana or three gins and tonic on a hot day. I don't remember anything more.

CHAPTER TWENTY–SIX

'I can't understand how they could have let you do it,' Louise said.

'Who?'

'Vivien Leigh and that idiot Finch, of course. It was just madness.'

'They couldn't have stopped me. I was in the grip of a higher power.'

Louise laughed. 'In the grip of whisky more likely. The highest power you know is Johnnie Walker.'

'Might have been a bit of that in it, but there was more to it. I'll tell you one thing though, that's the last firewalking I'll go to.'

I was in bed in my hotel room in Kandy four days after the firewalking. I'd collapsed immediately after getting off the coals and been taken to hospital with second-degree burns to the soles of my feet and a wound in my back. I'd been sedated for the first few days while they worked on the damage. Someone had sent for Louise and she'd taken a few days' leave to nurse me. There's nothing like a professional nurse to make you comfortable, especially when she'll let you take a few liberties with her person and offer you relief in more ways than one. Thanks to my much-abused but excellent constitution I was mending fast and it wouldn't be long before I'd be able to try a step or two. I have to admit I wasn't looking forward to that. My feet were still very, very tender, but Louise said I had to get back on them for the sake of my confidence, ligaments, etc.

We'd been talking non-stop since I came out of the morphine. She'd heard about my exploit with the elephant and declared herself proud of me. That was a strange note for Louise to strike and several times I'd caught her looking at me in an odd way. I'd told her what Ranu and I had been up to with Grace, just so she wouldn't get any wrong ideas about me. She still seemed to think that I'd been brave rather than desperate and terrified. I didn't work too hard at disabusing her.

'They didn't come to see you in the hospital,' she said. 'I thought they might at least have done that.'

'I guess they had their own agenda. They've gone, have they?'

'Yes. Well, I suppose it wouldn't have mattered, seeing that you were delirious most of the time.'

'I wasn't delirious. Not ever.'

'You were so. I've learned a lot about you, Richard Browning. You're a big softie, really.'

I didn't like the drift of this conversation. 'What about Finch and Vivien?'

'They've gone to Los Angeles. I understand she had hysterics and they had to knock her out to get her on the plane.'

I shook my head. 'Like Dana Andrews said, "Not a happy person."'

'He came in briefly, too. I quite liked him. He left you a bottle of what he called snake oil.'

'Let's see.'

She produced a cardboard box containing a bottle of Jack Daniel's and a few copies of *Variety* and the *Hollywood Reporter*. Louise saw the way I looked at the package.

'Miss it, do you, Dick?'

'It's an insane place, full of phonies and hustlers. But yes, I do miss it.'

Two days later I got a notice from the British and Foreign bank in Colombo that the sum of four thousand pounds had been credited to my account. With my last payment for work on the movie plus the bonus this meant I had near enough to six thousand pounds in hand with only a few medical expenses and a hotel bill to pay. As far as I could recall, apart from very brief times in Hollywood (and that's leaving aside the debts), this was the most affluent I'd ever been. I decided to celebrate by taking my first steps. I should have waited until Louise was there but I was feeling full of confidence. I lifted my legs from the bed and placed my still heavily bandaged feet on the floor. Very gently I eased myself up until I was standing straight, or very nearly so. Not too bad.

I took one small step and made it okay. Another. So far so good. I got bold, stepped out a bit and screamed as the pain hit me. Maybe it was the blood getting through or the skin stretching, I don't know, but it felt as if red-hot needles were being driven into my soles. I crawled back onto the bed, ripped the top from Andrews' bottle and took a long swig. I shuddered and waited for the bourbon to do some good. I was worried. They'd assured me the feet would heal up but what if they were wrong? There aren't too many movie parts for men on crutches. I took another drink and started to feel a little better. I'd just gone at it too early and without help. Louise would know the tricks.

The phone rang. *Speak of the devil*, I thought as I snatched it up. 'Hello, honey.'

'Honey? What's with this honey. You turning fag these days, Dick?'

'Bobby! Jesus, I didn't expect . . . Oww!' I yelled as I bumped my right foot against the bed end.

'The hell you screaming for? You okay?'

'I've burned my feet. It's a long story.'

'While you were working on the movie?'

'No. After it finished.'

'Pity. Can't do anything on the insurance. So, you're not busy planting tea or anything like that?'

'What is this, Bobby? You don't pay for a long distance call just to chat. Don't worry, you'll get your commission. It won't be much, I was just a sort of technical assistant.'

'We can talk about that when you get here. When can you leave?'

He explained that Vivien had had a breakdown on arriving in Hollywood and that she'd been unable to complete her work on the film. It was a big budget picture for the time and the studio had invested too much in it to allow it to die, so they were going to cast another actress and do a lot of reshooting.

'Who?' I asked.

'You'll never guess. Liz Taylor.'

'Jesus. She's too young and too . . .'

'Sexy? Come on, Dick. This is Hollywood. How can a broad be too young and too sexy?'

I knew Bobby Silk wouldn't have read the script because he never read anything except the trade papers and contracts. I told him that in the movie Finch got drunk and played bicycle polo rather than go upstairs to fuck his wife.[38]

'So, they got a problem there. Point is, they want you back to help them get it right. This guy Finch says he needs you and he's calling some of the shots. I can negotiate you some good bucks, Dick, and they'll pay for your ticket out. Whaddya say?'

This was obviously Finch's way of doing something for me and I was touched. It was never wise to take Bobby Silk at his word, though, and I pressured him for more details.

'Seems they got some elephant work they think you can help with.'

'They've done all that.'

'Like I say, they gotta do it again. Hey, this is costing me, Dick. Are you in or out?'

Elephants or not, there was no good pretending, not with the bourbon warm in my veins and the *Hollywood Reporters* sitting there with a picture of Rita Hayworth on the front page. Although I was surprised to find that she wasn't really better-looking than Louise. 'I guess I'm in.'

'Great. Make it as quick as you can, baby. Liz Taylor. You play your cards right, this could lead to something big for you.'

'Sure. Bobby, ah, is Johnny Stompanato around these days?'

'Nah. I hear he's in Vegas working for Mickey[39] and the boys. Why?'

'Never mind. I'll be there as quick as I can.'

'Ciao.'

I was in a thoughtful mood when Louise got back. She was still wearing her nurse's outfit, which has never been a particular interest of mine, but Louise looked good in everything. The ceiling fan wasn't keeping the room very cool and she stripped off her dress, causing my interest to mount considerably. She noticed.

'You're well and truly on the mend, I see.'

'Tried to walk,' I grunted. 'Screamed and fell over.'

'Huh.' She was down to her bra and panties now and fanning herself with a copy of the *Colombo Times*. 'I suppose you went about it all the wrong way. Just tried to walk, did you?'

'Sure.'

'Idiot. You have to test out the foot bit by bit, heel, sole and toe. No wonder it hurt like hell. I'll show you later. Let's have a look at them.'

She removed the bandages. She would have made a great safe-cracker, Louise, or a bomb-defuser. She had the gentlest of touches. 'Hmm. Looking good. You'll be all right to hobble about soon.'

'When?'

I must have spoken sharply because she shot me a funny look. 'Couple of days. Why?'

Suddenly, I didn't want to pack up and go back to LA on my own with all that money in my pocket. Back to more money and perhaps some real success at last. To do what? Chase starlets, console divorcees? What was the point? I reached out and took Louise's hand. It was firm and strong from all that hard nursing work and tennis. I had a powerful need to hang on to her.

'I'm going back to Hollywood. I've got a job there and I've got a fair bit of money in hand. It's a hell of a place to be with no dough.'

'Yes?'

'How would you like to come with me?'

She stopped fanning and put the paper on the bed. 'To do what?'

'Whatever you like. Travel around. Live together. Get married.'

She stared at me. 'You're serious?'

'I am. We get on well together and I've got very sore feet.'

She laughed, leaned forward and kissed me. The touch and feel and smell of her got me right back in the mood. She took off her underwear and I slid down on the bed and she moved on top of me, being careful to keep well clear of my feet. We managed, did pretty well in fact. Afterwards, she accepted an inch of Jack Daniel's with water.

'Is this what we'll be drinking?'

'You'll come?'

'Do you think much about the future, Dick?'

If I'd been honest I would have admitted that I thought more about the past, but that would have made me sound middle-aged, or worse. 'Not much.'

'I do, especially lately. Take a look at this.' She folded the paper so I could read an item about the Americans testing a hydrogen bomb. 'Those bastards are going to blow us all up. I'm sure of it. If not them, then the Russians. I don't want to go back to Sydney to marry Doctor James Talbot and have three kids and live on the north shore. I want to have some *fun!*'

So that's what we did.

NOTES

1. *Crossfire,* RKO, 1947; *King Solomon's Mines,* MGM, 1950; *Quo Vadis,* MGM, 1951; *Viva Zapata!* C20th Fox, 1952; *The Winslow Boy,* Eagle Lion, 1950; *The Wooden Horse,* Wessex, 1950; *The Lavender Hill Mob,* Ealing, 1951.
2. See *'Box Office' Browning.*
3. An Australian expression referring to an unbranded or semi-wild bull difficult to control. Mallee scrub is rough country in the north-west of Victoria.
4. See *Browning Battles On.*
5. Browning seems to have forgotten that it was his decision to work with Flynn in *Sante Fe Trail* rather than pursue a role in the David O. Selznick epic. At the time his friendship with Flynn looked likely to advance his career. See *Browning in Buckskin,* p. 196 and *Browning PI,* pp. 1–4.
6. The hero of a series of novels by 'Sapper' (H. C. MacNeile and later G. T. Fairlie) about Captain Hugh Drummond, an imperialist vigilante.
7. Browning refers, somewhat uncharitably, to Leslie Howard Stainer, who was born in London to immigrant Hungarian parents and, more accurately, to Larushka Skikne, born in Lithuania and raised in South Africa, both of whom achieved success in films as poised English types.
8. When performing in radio plays in Sydney, Finch would have followed the then standard practice of wearing evening dress.

Usually, but not always, a studio audience was present. The actors wore formal attire in either case.

9. Johnny Stompanato was the bodyguard of Los Angeles gangster Mickey Cohen and the lover of film star Lana Turner. In 1958 he was stabbed to death in mysterious circumstances by Cheryll Crane, Lana Turner's daughter. It sounds as if Browning was keeping dangerous company, and his departure from Hollywood in 1952 might have been due to more pressing problems than unpaid rent.

10. According to his biographer, Olivier stood five feet ten inches. See Donald Spotto, *Laurence Olivier,* HarperCollins, London, 1991, p. 26. Spotto also confirms Olivier's bisexuality, see pp. 196–8.

11. Olivier, in fact, was forty-four, twelve years younger than Browning. Photographs, however, confirm Browning's observation. Olivier was grey at the temples and frequently wore half glasses; snapshots of Browning show him to have had a full head of dark hair, a trim figure and a remarkably, given his manner of life, unlined, clean-shaven face.

12. Another example of Browning's remarkable memory. Agatha Christie's novel, featuring her Belgian detective Hercule Poirot, *Mrs McGinty's Dead,* was indeed published by Collins in 1952.

13. For more accurate information on Browning's military service in the two world wars, see *'Box Office' Browning,* and *Browning PI.*

14. See *'Beverly Hills' Browning,* p. 217 and *Browning Takes Off,* pp. 1-5.

15. Presumably, Browning means Restoration plays. His knowledge of the history of the theatre was far from good, but his description appears to fit the works of Sheridan, Congreve, Wycherley, etc.

16. Niven makes the remark in his memoir *Bring on the Empty Horses,* London, 1975. Peter Finch died of a massive heart

attack in 1977, which helps to fix the date of Browning's recording of this passage of his chequered career.

17. See especially *Browning PI*.

18. *See 'Box Office' Browning*.

19. In the final version of the film there is no European nurse, nor is there a policeman. It is likely that these characters appeared in the draft Grace Drewe and Browning read but not in the shooting script.

20. Another indication that Browning had been involved in some trouble back in Hollywood. Gambling was the most likely cause.

21. In fact, *The Best Years Of Our Lives* won five Academy awards. It is generally accepted that the heavy promotion schedule Finch embarked on to promote the film *Network* and his own Oscar prospects, contributed to his death. He was awarded the Oscar posthumously.

22. The once-popular theory that the Vedda, dark-skinned hunter-gatherers who used bows and arrows and throwing sticks, were the progenitors of the Australian Aborigines has long since been discounted. South-East Asia is now thought to be the source of the migration of the Aborigines, at least 50,000 years ago.

23. See *'Beverly Hills' Browning*, pp. 39–96.

24. To date, no record of Browning's activities in the Caribbean has emerged. As noted in earlier volumes of his memoirs, his recording methods were inaccurate and it is possible that when more cassettes are transcribed this reference will become clear.

25. It was some years after Browning's death before a militant part of the Tamil protest movement in Sri Lanka adopted this name. Browning's choice of it here must be a complete coincidence.

26. For Browning's lifelong enmity towards Hughes see *'Box Office' Browning*.

27. Browning reveals here his very shaky literary grasp. Sherlock Holmes was, of course, the creation of Arthur Conan Doyle. Dr John Watson is the fictional narrator of the stories.

28. Browning refers, presumably, to Trader Faulkner and Elaine Dundey, authors respectively of *Peter Finch: A Biography* Angus & Robertson, London, 1979 and *Finch, Bloody Finch,* Michael Joseph, London, 1980.

29. Dieterle (1897-1973) spanned the silent and talking picture era and was still working in Hollywood in the late 1950s when colour and stereophonic sound arrived. His best-known films are the rather dull 'biopics' *Zola and Pasteur,* as well as *Rope of Sand, Peking Express* and *The Turning Point.*

30. In fact, Browning was fifty-seven years of age when these events occurred. He was so given to concealing how old he was that he may have actually forgotten that he was *exactly* three times Ranu Pelham-Smith's age.

31. No such dialogue occurs in the released version of the film, but it was subject to so much editing and reshooting that the scene Browning describes is likely to have been omitted.

32. Browning was partly right. *The Three Musketeers* (1974) and *The Four Musketeers* (1975), directed by Richard Lester, were shot simultaneously. The position with regard to the Superman movies is less clear. TV versions of the various films include footage from the others and out-takes.

33. Browning has his chronology somewhat confused. *The Nun's Story* was not made until some years after *Elephant Walk,* but it bore the similarity of Finch, cast as a doctor, combating an epidemic.

34. Presumably *Duel in the Jungle* (1954), a US/UK co-production that starred Jeanne Craine and Wilfred Hyde-White with Andrews.

35. A film about the exploits and death of General Gordon entitled *Khartoum* was made in 1966 with Charlton Heston in the title

role. Browning's name does not appear in the credits. *Burke and Wills,* a Hoyts-Edgley production of 1985, starred Jack Thompson in the role Browning would have thought of for himself—the doomed explorer Charles O'Hara Burke. Browning's remark is interesting as it reflects his continued attachment to the country of his birth.

36. See *'Box Office' Browning,* pp. 130–5.

37. In fact, Caine says, 'A little bit of God goes a very long way with me.'

38. Film citics agree that the casting of the young and beautiful Elizabeth Taylor doomed *Elephant Walk.* It was impossible to believe that a virile man of Finch's stamp could resist her under the spell of his father and his obligation to his 'guests'.

39. Presumably Mickey Cohen, Hollywood gangster and associate of major organised crime figures.

www.ingramcontent.com/pod-product-compliance
Lightning Source LLC
Chambersburg PA
CBHW061222170626
46809CB00007B/2553